Butcher the Doll

Charlie Rogers

Published by Charlie Rogers, 2024.

BUTCHER THE DOLL

First edition. April 8, 2024.

ISBN: 979-8224686407

Written by Charlie Rogers.

Table of Contents

This is for everyone who ever believed in me.

one. BULL

Rain batters both our faces, mine and the dead man's.

I've been chasing this thief all night, down grimy alleyways and through streets crowded with both humans and other droids, out to where the city's neon hum is barely audible. Now there's no more running, no more pleading. The wiry young man's final expression is oddly placid, his eyes more resigned than frantic, despite the trickle of blood still leaking from the finger-sized hole I blasted through his skull. Frigid water soaks through my jacket onto my synthetic skin as I study him.

This is my last kill.

I tell myself this same lie every time: when Chiang gives me an assignment, while I track down my target, and after, surveying my morbid handiwork. But I don't know how to do anything else. I was designed to kill, programmed for it. It's all I've ever done.

On the horizon, a smudge of ashy gray wedges between distant mountains—a place I'll never see—and the oily, starless sky, indicating that morning approaches.

I snap a holo of the splayed corpse with my tablet—Chiang likes proof of all her Butchers' completed kills—and try not to think about how many hundreds of similar images crowd the memory on my handheld device. Blood spatter and blank, unseeing eyes, more emotionless than the robotic models whirring in my face. I'm not programmed to feel remorse. And yet—

I turn towards home. As much as I have one.

I trudge along long-abandoned train tracks, the uneven ties preferable to sloshing mud. The rain pouring from my permanently stubbly scalp is frustrating, but, as long as I keep moving, it's not too cold. There's a portable heating unit in my tent that should warm me up quick once I'm out of these sopping clothes.

On the outskirts of town, I pass a derelict building with a line of Butchers sleeping against its crumbling front wall. They aren't Chiang's, so I don't recognize any of them, though two of the older, less human-looking models are identical to each other. They're the same make as Stone, who is as close to a mentor-figure for me as any Butcher has ever had. The others all look like

1

people—brutish, overly muscular, ill-tempered people—and each sports a long scar along his right cheek. We all do.

There's something calming about their rain-slicked, slack faces in their down cycles, though walking past them feels a bit like stumbling across a pack of sleeping dogs. I know I have nothing to fear from them, not unless a turf war breaks out between Chiang—the self-described queen of the underworld—and whoever owns these droids. Chiang quashed the last challenge so mercilessly I doubt any of the other kingpins will be angling to take her out any time soon.

It's not fear that I feel, but envy.

Butchers don't usually feel cold, or pain, or much of anything at all. They can sleep in the freezing rain, same as they could a soft mattress in a warm room. Not me. Chiang jokes that I'm defective—one wrong move away from retirement—easily replaced by a more efficient new model. When she makes that joke, her laugh is always accompanied by a tell: her eyes flit to the left. I doubt she knows she does it. It tells me she's keeping me around for another reason, not just because I'm as effective as all her other killers. I'm her secret weapon, a Butcher who understands pain from both sides.

Tonight, I don't want to be special. I want to be warm.

It takes an hour of walking—past the crumbling slums and through the neon thrum of downtown—to reach the rows of tents and makeshift shelters on the opposite end of town. Quiet. The sun's not quite risen, so no reason for the human denizens of this indigent village to wake up yet, to shuffle off to their menial jobs or panhandling. Sometimes runaway droids will try to hide out here—Dolls and Sous and Utties and whatever other specialties our creators decide to assign us—but they always get found. I've had to drag a few back myself, terminate a few others.

I let one slip away once, a diminutive old Uttie named Ediick with a malfunctioning leg. Chiang had hinted I should let this one go, suggesting a sentimentality I rarely witness from her. So I did. Told him to follow the tracks to the mountains, and I remember his wide eyes, alive with both desperation and gratitude, as he limped away, glancing back to confirm I wasn't about to shoot him in the spine. His tiny figure merged into the shadows beneath the overpass. Sometimes I wonder if he ever made it there, what sort of life a rundown ex-Uttie could find in the hills.

Quentin—a rare human who doesn't cower in fear at my presence—sits cross-legged in the space between his tent and mine, underneath a huge rainbow-colored umbrella balanced against his shoulder. He grins when he sees me, his skin crinkling like yellowed paper around his playful eyes. "Bring me any meat, Mr. Butcherman?"

I'm not programmed to smile, but Quentin has helped me learn how. I try it now, the edges of my mouth quivering upwards, resisting my commands at first. By the time I've ducked into the shelter of my tent, I think it might look genuine. "Did you stay up all night watching my tent?" I crouch in the low doorway, facing him.

Quentin sighs. "Sure did, Mr. Butcherman."

He knows I have no way to pay him for the favor. We've been neighbors in the unhoused encampment for years. Even when the vicebots sweep through to kick us out, forcing us to separate and resettle, he always finds me again to claim the spot next to mine. I think he would say we're friends.

"You didn't have to do that, you know." I peel off my jacket and shake it out into the rain, careful not to spray too much onto Quentin.

He doesn't seem to mind. Nothing bothers him except the story he sometimes tells me about the senseless slaughter of his wife and son, decades earlier. *Too old to do much 'bout it now*, he told me. *They're all dead anyway, the people that done it.* His gray eyes burned red before he collected himself.

Not tonight, though. Tonight, he's all smiles. "Got nothin' better to do."

I crawl deeper into my tent and set my weapon on the edge of my bed. Next off is my shirt. I toss it aside and grab a rag to blot the wetness from my chest and arms, then wring out my shirt onto the pavement, positioning myself so Quentin can only see my forearms. They appear remarkably human, down to the fine hairs that stand at attention in the cold. I peek my head out. "You could have slept like everyone else."

He shakes his head. "I like it quiet like this. None of them squawkin' ladies or barkin' dogs. I close my eyes, you know, I can still hear them trains that used to run by here." He gazes wistfully towards the surrounding camp, a row of soggy cardboard boxes arranged into a sad village. His smile wavers. "Rememberin' is all I got."

I peel off my uncomfortably drenched pants and squeeze as much as I can out of them. They're won't dry in time for me to wear them again. Quentin stares at me, a hollow version of his usual grin propped onto his tired face, and I realize he can see more of me than I'm comfortable showing. Exhaustion and desperation to remove my wet clothes caused me to forget myself. I feel a rush of embarrassment and duck from his view.

"I used to be fit like you." Quentin's voice is wistful from the other side of the nylon barrier separating us. "Not that you'd know it now."

I hear footsteps: heavy, familiar.

From a small bag by my mattress, I grab my sleeping clothes—Quentin calls them my *peejays*, and I've never asked him what that means—and yank on the soft plaid shorts with a torn leg. Before pulling on my equally worn white tanktop, I check the opening. Dock lumbers into view.

"Go inside." I point to the unzipped entrance of Quentin's tent.

Quentin salutes me before closing his ridiculous umbrella. He clambers into his tent and peers out like a spy.

Dock, Chiang's newest Butcher and full-time errand droid, climbs into my tiny home without invitation, dripping water everywhere. For an instant, he registers surprise at the sight of me—even though he obviously came here looking for me—but his face quickly returns to its slack resting position. "Chiang wants to see you."

I meet his narrowed, dark-violet eyes. "Chiang can fuck off. I was out all night on her last assignment." I realize the confusion I caught flickering across his face was because no one ever sees me out of my jacket. I push down the shame of being caught with my shirt off, as if I'm as immodest as any other Butcher.

Dock registers no response as he wipes the water from the sleeves of his shiny charcoal-colored jacket onto my floor. "You shouldn't talk about the boss like that, Bull." His nose looks like it's been broken in five places—bulbous, misshapen and off-center—but he's too young to have found that much trouble. They designed him this way. Whoever's building us has a very strange sense of humor.

"If it's not urgent, I'm going to sleep first. Tell Chiang I need my beauty rest." I settle onto my mattress.

Again, no reaction. Butchers have zero sense of humor. Quentin tells me I'm a riot, but only by accident. I can tell when *he's* joking, though, which is

4

another reason the other Butchers—except for Stone—don't accept me. None of us ever laugh, but I sometimes know I should.

After a long pause, Dock nods. "I'll tell her. If she's not happy—"

I turn up my little heater and stretch across my lumpy bed. "I've known Chiang a lot longer than you. She just wants to give me another assignment, which I won't do until tonight anyway. She's keeping you busy so she doesn't have to look at your fucked-up face."

Dock's hand rises to his face, two fingers running along the bumpy bridge of his nose. "My face is—"

"Get out of here, Dock."

The sight of this beast of a machine, all muscles and menace, trying to fit himself back through the tiny opening of my tent brings the beginnings of an involuntary smile to my face. A vibration in my chest feels like an unexpressed laugh, like it's a gesture I once knew, buried in my programming somewhere. I wonder if all Butchers have latent emotions or if I really am, as Chiang says, a walking defect.

Once he's gone, I pull up a single threadbare blanket, squeezing the butt of my gun tucked half under my chest, and close my eyes.

The rain hasn't stopped for weeks. It streaks my window, washing the dull sunrise into a charcoal shimmer. I suck on my pink vaportube—its bitter epi buried under sticky sweetness on my tongue—then tap it against the pane, tilting my chin towards the heavens. "You can quit this rainy bullshit any time now, you know."

"Mix, you talking to God again?" A honeyed voice purrs from behind me.

I turn. Jemmi leans against my doorjamb, grinning, in a pose I'm sure her clients find irresistible. A turquoise robe glides over her curves like a restless tide. Despite the foundation she's already applied, a hint of a bruise on her right cheek peeks through, enough that I know she's not really trying to hide it from me. She has the same back-alley tech I do, the implant that scrambles pain into pleasure—which I recommend to all the Dolls working here—but still it angers me to see her perfect face sullied. She smiles as if nothing's amiss.

"Not *my* god. My creator—well, my designer anyway—was a scrawny weirdo. Did I ever tell you I met him?" I beckon for her to join me, waving my vaportube in her direction.

She shakes her head as she assumes the spot next to me, extending an open hand to borrow my v. It's almost finished anyway, so I hand it off to let her kick it. My robe falls open so she reaches for my penis instead, as if she doesn't see hundreds like it every week. I cluck in disapproval and tug my robe shut.

"No fun." She takes the vaportube with a trouble-making grin.

It annoys me when she treats me like a client, but she's relatively new here, at least compared to me. I've been here since my incept, working for Chiang, though I've only had this room for three years. The previous occupant, a schemer named Toyo, ran off with three younger female Dolls from downstairs. The next day, two Butchers brought them all back and painted the lobby with Toyo's circuits. The other failed escapees went back to work, and I, the senior-most male Doll in the shop, inherited this room. On the half-clock days the sun makes it through the clouds, it's a charming closet of a room. Today, it's gloomy.

The vaportube gurgles as Jemmi draws from it. She runs both her hands along its length like she's trying to tease a client towards climax, then pulls it away. Wisps of not-smoke trickle from the edge of her perfectly formed lips, but I can't take my eyes off the bruise.

"You met... fuck, I can't remember your creator's name." Jemmi offers the v back to me but I wave it away. She has a terrible memory for details, which I suspect has held her back in cultivating a stable of regulars.

"Everett. Thoroughly average in every way. Except his brain, I guess. I was trawling the streets back then, ripe for plucking. He pulled up in his porto—biggest I've ever seen—like a proper john." I drag my finger across the window, vaguely pointing to the eastern slum where he found me. "Honey, it was dreadful. His cock was shaped like a fishhook and he kept whispering *I made you, I made you.* The most annoyingly existential hour of my existence."

Jemmi tilts her head towards the blurry mountains in the distance. "I don't know who made me."

"Girl." I reach back to the nightstand drawer where I keep my vaportubes. I pass up yellow, red and another pink, before snatching a purple v. My favorite. "They use machines to make us now. There's a whole-ass factory downtown just for Sous."

She doesn't seem to be listening.

"Depressing as hell, but it smells divine, like they're baking cookies in there." I press the v to my lips but don't yet inhale. "Just like mama used to make."

It's a play on an in-joke we have in this house. When one of us complains about the depraved situations some of our clients force us into, another Doll will always pipe up with *just like Daddy used to do,* which we all think is hilarious after all these years. But it flies over Jemmi's head.

"Okay, what's going on in that gorgeous trap of a brain?" I stroke the gossamer material hovering at the precipice of her shoulder, tugging it down to bare more pale flesh, then pull it back up to her clavicle.

Jemmi still doesn't look at me, her gaze drifting somewhere between the mountains and the disappointing glow of the should-be sun. "Do you ever think about freedom?"

I haven't told her my plan. Maybe when I'm ready to make my move. Maybe. For now, no one knows.

"Every day." I drag on the v; the insides of my mouth tingle with its tartness, but still that bitterness lingers underneath. "Only people who don't think about freedom are already free."

She shakes the pink tube she's still holding and lifts it to the light. "So you never... accept this?"

I stroke my knuckles around her mottled bruise. She doesn't flinch.

"It's not so bad, love. Listen to the stories your johns tell after they've cum. Loveless unions. Grinding, crushing boredom. They're not as free as they think they are." I follow her gaze to the mountains and wonder, as I do every morning, what lies beyond that ridge.

Jemmi knows I'm lying but nods anyway. She draws a quick inhale and instantly brightens up. "So who is it tonight?"

I grin. "My big floppy whale."

She scrunches her face—I resist the urge to remind her that we *do* age, despite what the humans believe, and she should be careful not to screw up her best asset—and sighs. "You sure Wade doesn't ever want a girl? Maybe bring a droid home to Mama?"

"He's a kingpin. I doubt he's got a mama at home baking pies." I draw from the vaportube, savoring the tartness.

Jemmi lowers herself to the edge of my bed and tightens the sash of her robe as if the material isn't translucent. "I've asked this before... doesn't he have his own Dolls? Why's he lining Chiang's pockets?"

Wade tapped two fingers across my abs like he was playing a long-forgotten musical instrument. "First rule of business, handsome. Don't cum where you eat. Too messy." He grinned.

If I didn't already know, I'd never have pegged Wade for a kingpin. A wiry little guy with a huge cock and an off-kilter grin, he looked like a low-lev, someone counting chits in some vapory basement, not the guy who'd be running a mini-empire. The sort of character who'd justify his seedy dealings—it's all for my family—not swinging by a rival's brothel once or twice a week to swap fucks with a droid.

"Oh, is that how the saying goes?"

He slid one of his hands down to gently grip my flaccid penis even though I knew he was done for the night. His expression morphed from mischievous to earnest. "I have a plan, Mix. A plan to get out. I could buy you out—Chiang owes me a Doll—and you could come with me if you want."

I thought about telling him I don't eat where I cum but, instead, I smiled. "I'd like that."

I shoot Jemmi a withering look, then use both hands to gesture to my near-nakedness. "You think any of his broke-down Dolls can compete with *this*?"

She laughs. Something outside catches her attention and the laugh trails off, replaced by that same faraway look. I think it's likely just the sky—her room's window faces a wall—and I'm about to turn to confirm that theory when I spot a growing shadow on my open door.

Dock, Chiang's latest hench-droid, fills the doorway. He's here to collect her sizable cut of our earnings, as he does every week.

"You're early, Dock." It would be easy for me to grab my tablet from the drawer, but it's more fun to bust this Butcher's chops. I'd heard rumors they were starting to give Butchers personalities—though I can't imagine who'd want that feature in a killdroid—and Dock is proof. It's not *much* of a personality, but he's infinitely more fun to fuck with than his predecessor.

Jemmi turns to him, allowing the strap of her nightgown to slip so one of her breasts nearly makes an appearance. We all amuse ourselves by fucking with Butchers. If they haven't been sent to kill you, they're like monstrously large, monstrously dumb dogs. Jemmi's strategy, as always, is to flirt. "Hi, Dock."

Dock isn't flustered by her efforts; his deep-set indigo eyes still show no expression. "Clear out, Jemmi. Me and Mix have business." He steps into the room. "I'll get your take later."

"No need to be rude." Jemmi huffs but I know she isn't bothered either. We all play these games to get through the day. She rests both her hands on his huge chest as she passes. "Don't be too long, sweetie. I'm *waiting*."

Once she's gone, Dock closes the door. He clears his throat but doesn't say anything.

I reach into the drawer and fish out my tablet from beneath the novelty jockstraps last night's trick wanted us to wear. By the time I turn, I find Dock has already removed his shirt. "What's this?"

"I need a, uh, draining." He sounds shy, which might be adorable if he weren't an implacable killing machine.

BUTCHER THE DOLL

Butchers are constructed with a disturbing design flaw. They possess no sex drive and can't experience pleasure, but they are equipped with working genitals, and larger-than-average endowments, in proportion with their massive frames. If they don't drain their testicles a few times a year, they'll malfunction. I shudder to think *why* they're constructed with working sex organs, because I know the answer, and it's disturbing.

I roll my eyes. "You don't need to undress. This isn't a date."

He ignores me, stripping off his pants. Once he's naked, I beckon him closer. "You know I'm the most expensive Doll in this whole house. You could—"

He cuts me off. "You're not afraid of me."

I take his cock into my hand. It instantly inflates to full size. Dock pushes me away. "Was that it? That felt weird."

I've wondered before what Butchers actually *feel*. It's certainly not that their bodies are numb or they lack tactile nerves. They feel *something*; it's just not anything I can understand, same as they can't comprehend what humans or every other class of droid experience as pleasure and pain. I also wonder if their emotions are similar, like the rumble of someone shouting in another room.

"It's your first time?" Obviously, it's his first time. He's only a few months old and has perhaps never sported an erection before now.

He grunts a response, and if I didn't know better, I'd think I've embarrassed him.

"Lay down. It takes a tick or two." I point to the bed. It's been years since I've had to drain a Butcher; it's easy work as long as they don't try to fuck me—all they know how to do is inflict pain—but it's inefficient to hire me, at the top of my game, when they could pick any Doll off the street and let the incessant rain wash away their mess.

I suspect Chiang is testing me. Why, or for what, I don't know. Soon, it won't matter.

three. BULL

I t's dark again. I wake to find the rain has slowed, based on the pattering against the worn orange fabric of my tent.

I close my eyes; I open them and eight hours have vanished, dull sunlight transformed into expansive black in an instant. Droids don't dream. Quentin sometimes tells me about his dreams, unaware that it's a foreign concept to me.

I grab a new shirt from the bag by my bed. It's been sitting near the heater all day, so it's warm against my skin, offsetting the chilling air leaking through my tent's busted zipper. The pants are still wet, heavy and uncomfortable once I pull them back on.

Chiang grants me a small stipend, so I'll go buy some new clothes tomorrow. I only own four black T-shirts—identical except for the varying ways they're unraveling—and a single pair of black pants. Everything's falling apart and smells of rust.

I strap on my weapon and crawl through the opening of my tent, expecting a cheerful greeting from Quentin.

His tent is gone. In its place is a dark kidney-shaped stain on the pavement that could be blood or could be old oil. I glance around to see if he's changed locations, but I can't think why he would have.

It's not the first time he's disappeared like this. Usually he warns me when he's going out scavenging for food, but usually I downcycle at night, not during the day. I'm not sure when he sleeps at all.

I convince myself that the stain must have been here before us—if it's fresh blood, the rain would wash it away—and Quentin is fine. He'll likely be back by the time I return from whatever errand Chiang has lined up for me.

I duck back into my tent and gather all my clothes plus assorted belongings—my gun-cleaning kit and a multi-colored glass marble I found in a gutter—into a clear plastic satchel. One of Chiang's Utties will wash the clothes for me while I'm on tonight's errand, but if I left them, they'd be too easy to steal. My heater and my mattress and the tent itself have to stay, though, even though Quentin isn't here to guard them for me. I have to trust that most people, even my most desperate neighbors, are smart enough not to risk robbing a Butcher.

13

I weave through other tents on my way to Chiang's building, ignoring all the widened eyes glaring at me, the mother who collects her small children from my path. Based on the level of activity, I guess it's just past sundown, dinnertime for most people. A ponytailed man cooks unrecognizable meat on a makeshift grill, and the smell both nauseates and entices me. Sous are the only family of droids who crave human food, and none of us require organic sustenance, though all of us *can* consume it. It isn't the smoky aroma of bubbling fat that compels me, but the smell of death.

Ponytail glares at me, defiance masking terror, his limbs locked in fear. Behind him a toddler plucks the stringy white hair from a plastic doll's head.

"Enjoy." I gesture toward the meat skewered over a fire inside a metal barrel. If I had confidence that my smile would ever look friendly and not terrifying, I would try easing his panic with a simple disarming grin, the sort humans do without even trying. But my smile is a work in progress, so I nod and continue on.

Once I've cleared the overpass, the rainy, neon-lit streets fall quiet. During the day, they teem with people, self-absorbed humans staring at their wrist tablets, filing in and out of the glass towers. But at night, all those bodies return to the residential units on the other side of town and the business district becomes deserted.

I listen to my rhythmic footsteps, heavy soles striking wet pavement. The submetro rumbles underneath the sidewalk like a hungry demon. I gaze up at the sky through a gap in the towers, cold mist meeting my face. Another starless night. The rain's not letting up any time soon.

A few blocks from Chiang's high-rise, a woman's scream shatters the placid evening, echoing around me. I stop and turn.

She runs toward me, a mass of frizzy green hair obscuring her features, a long coat slapping at her legs. One of her shoes is missing. The sharp scent of her desperation tickles the back of my skull, and I reach for my weapon.

Behind her, an implacable silhouette looms.

"Help me!" She sees me, but isn't close enough to really *see* me through the mist.

I unclip my gun—how many times have I heard that subtle pop?—and raise it in her direction. She's close enough for me to fire on, but it's not my kill.

A single gunshot: its sound bounces around me like frantic music.

The woman crashes to the sidewalk with a muted thud.

Her killer lowers his weapon, clipping it to his belt as he approaches. Stone. A potential smile twitches at the edge of my mouth, aching to form.

"Thanks for the assist." Stone kicks the woman's body so she faces the sky. "Wasn't necessary."

I gaze down at the woman, at the wet strands of hair obscuring half her face. Her fear still lingers in my nostrils. "What'd this one do?"

He snaps a holo with two muted clicks then kicks her over again to document his killing blast. "Didn't ask. You seeing Chiang?"

Stone's the oldest Butcher I know, one of the oldest models still in operation. Unlike me or most of the other Butchers on the street, he only resembles a human in passing, with silverish skin, a squared head and laser-red eyes. But he's also the only Butcher I've ever encountered who knows how to smile, before our creators deleted that from our programming.

He took me under his wing when I came online, a decade or so ago. He showed me where to power up and where our crew of Butchers powers down. When he discovered that I'm not immune to cold, he used his own stipend to secure the tent I still use.

I nod, and we start to walk. "She summoned me this morning. Been keeping me busy."

Stone's left leg wheezes with every step we take, popping on each impact with the concrete. "You'll be busier soon. That was my final kill."

I stop, cocking my head to the side. "Final kill?"

He pauses in a puddle, peering down at his reflection in the water, then wiggles his huge foot to disrupt it. He doesn't lift his head to face me when he speaks. "I'm on my way to retirement."

I shake my head. "No. You could run. I'll cover—"

Stone raises his hand to stop me. "Where would I go, Bull? To the hills? To do what? We only know how to do one thing." He glances around at the deserted buildings towering over us before continuing to walk. "Come on."

I follow him. "Stone, wait."

His leg continues: wheeze, pop. His other leg thuds the sidewalk, splashing through puddles. Early models were not designed for a modicum of stealth and even modern Butchers don't excel at it. Stone's told me that, in his early days, he was mostly used for public executions of political dissidents, before Chiang got into the business. He claims to have lost track of time but could be as old as fifty cycles.

The streets grow more crowded the closer we get to our destination, filled with ghoulish, blank-faced humans who all seem lost. There's too many of them for that to be true but I often wonder where they all come from, where they're going. No one lives around here except for Chiang.

"Don't be sentimental, Bull. It's inefficient." He pauses a few doors away from Chiang's tower. "But I'm glad I saw you tonight. There's no one else I'd rather spend my last few ticks with."

My eye twitches. "Glad? You know what that is?"

Stone smiles. A hideous approximation of one, but a smile nonetheless, and his eyes flicker like dying embers. "'Course I do." He presses a finger to his broad chest, above his pro-core. "Sometimes it's tough to understand what's going on in this ticker, but I *feel* plenty. You do too."

"Stone—"

He reaches for my forearm and squeezes. It hurts but I won't tell him that.

"It's time, Bull. It's time." Then he's moving again, and I follow, past the expressionless Butchers at the door, past Tie, the smiling Uttie who greets us at the elevator. We step inside.

Stone turns to me. "After I'm gone, ask Chiang about her husband."

"What?"

He smiles again. "Time for me to see whether there's another side for us."

The elevator door opens with a whoosh and a strangled beep.

Stone steps out without glancing back.

four. MIX

I sit at the window, waiting. It's so black outside that I can't differentiate the mountains from the air around them. I've heard murmurs of an encampment, somewhere in those hills, where escaped droids have made a life for themselves separate from their programming. I don't know if it's true, but I intend to find out.

It's been a slow day, by design. I try to keep the days I'm seeing Wade free of other appointments.

I tricked Dock into overpaying for his draining and almost felt bad about it—Butchers get shit stipends for their joyless existences—but I justified it to myself as a cleaning fee. He kept squirming and ended up making quite a mess. I left his account near-empty, so I doubt he'll be so extravagant next time—street Dolls are much cheaper—though I wouldn't mind. His awkward inexperience amused me. Maybe I'll offer him a discount next time.

After that, my afternoon client was easy. A sad widower named Otis who shows up every six months or so. He'll only hire me, no other Doll, and he requires so little effort that I figured it wouldn't create a conflict to see him on a Wade-day. I fucked him for about three ticks until he cried, then had to hold him as he sobbed for the remainder of an hour. It's always like that with poor Otis. I don't even think he's gay.

Jemmi and I went for a walk, but it's so horrible out there—both the weather and the scrabbling throngs of humanity outside, all desperate people pleading other desperate people for food, for shelter, for whatever it is that humans need. Love? I'm not sure I know what that is, but I know Dolls are capable of it. Sea and Skye, who used to share the room next to mine, were very much in love with one another despite being identical models. I miss them, Sea in particular. I told her not to risk a run without proper planning.

Since returning from the walk, all I've done is wait. Everyone else in the house is out trick-hunting, or if they're lucky, working with the johns they've found. I don't miss that hustle. Since I bagged Wade as a regular, I'm spared that hassle, though I'll still go out sometimes if I'm bored and have nothing on the books.

Wade is late, which is very unlike him. Usually he's early, sometimes annoyingly so. One time a few years ago, when he was first trying me out as his regular and I didn't yet have the resources to reserve so much time for him, Wade showed up as I was occupied with Rickey, an aggressive former boxer client of mine. I thought I'd blown it, but Wade was a good sport about the mixup. I never saw Rickey again and suspect Wade had him killed, but he's never owned up to it.

I draw from my vaportube and wet my lips, coating them in the vapor's tingling tanginess, then exhale against the window.

A loud knock rattles my door.

I tighten my robe. "Come in!"

One of Wade's Butchers clomps in. I don't know this one's name, but I'm sure it's something suitably aggressive like Stab, so that's what I call him. Stab ignores my saccharine greeting and sweeps the room—peering under the bed and into my narrow but fabulously deep closet—before clomping back into the hall.

A moment later, Stab returns, accompanied by another Butcher who I call Fist—he holds all the fingers of one hand together, a permanent malfunction—with Wade between them. It's comical how tiny he appears next to them.

"Mix, my sweet, my apologies." Wade impatiently waves the Butchers out of the room and slams the door behind them. "You know I hate to keep you waiting."

Wade pulls off his jacket and tosses it onto the small chair in the back of the room. He kicks off his shoes—losing even more height—then looks up at me with a devilish grin.

"Please, never apologize to me." I loop one finger into the knot of my robe's sash, ready to tease it apart.

Wade continues to strip, scattering his clothes around the room, and once he's down to his too-tight briefs, he pauses to eye me hungrily. I take him in as well.

Wade is not handsome, and in clothes, he seems unassuming. His dusty brown hair thins at the crown of his skull. His features are at best unremarkable and at worst mismatched, though his tar-black eyes lighten to a warm brown as he gets excited. The right side of his face is much more animated than the left, so he always seems a bit off-balance.

Once he removes his shirt, however, he reveals a well-defined physique that wouldn't be out of place on a Doll—if he was taller—but he never quite looks the part of a kingpin.

Wade bounds forward and hooks a few fingers into the belt of my robe, tugging me towards him. He cranes his neck up to kiss me, his mouth a mixture of tobacco and expensive liquor. Human luxuries.

"What are you in the mood for?" I slide my hand underneath the waistband of his crisp white underwear.

"The usual, handsome, the usual." Wade laughs—an unusual series of staccato, high-pitched bursts—and roughly tugs my robe open before yanking it off my shoulders. It flutters to the floor as he turns me around, bending me over the edge of my bed.

I grasp a tube of lubricant that I'd set on the bed and hand it back to him. I don't need it, but Wade likes how it feels, and I glance back as he tugs down the front of his briefs to let his cock flop out. He slathers the goopy lube on it and presses against me.

"I'm ready." I stretch out my arms to grasp the edges of the mattress.

He runs an oily hand along my back. "I don't want to hurt you." He says this every time.

"You can't hurt me." I crane my head back to meet his eyes, as bright and alive as they get. "But please don't try."

Wade laughs again, softer this time. I am reminded of my immense luck. Of all the Dolls in the city, including the ones he owns, Wade chose me. He's generous and surprisingly sexy, and most of all, gentle. Though it helps that my pain sensors are dialed down—thanks to my expensive tech—as he pushes himself all the way inside me. Sparklers hiss at the base of my skull—my implant translates intense pain into breathless ecstasy—as a humming pleasure spreads to my limbs like fire along a trail of accelerant.

Two ticks later, his breathing is frantic, grunting in surprise with every thrust as if he's never fucked before, before shuddering in a series of frantic yelps and collapsing on top of me.

This is the usual. It's no different than draining a Butcher, really. It wasn't always like this, but Wade's been starting this way for the better part of a year. We're not done, though.

He wipes off his drooling erection and climbs onto the bed, beckoning for me to join him. "Was that okay?"

I clamber up beside him, flashing a coy smile, and wrap my fist around his spongy, semi-flaccid cock. "You're my favorite."

That's not a lie. And not because I earn enough from him in a single night that I never need to trick-hunt, or that a man of his power could damage me with impunity but he chooses to be considerate. I really do like him. Just not as much as he likes me.

"You're just saying that." He reaches for my vaportube. The epi in it will rev him back up. When he breathes it in, the half-spent tube softly gurgling, I know he's already gearing up for another go. Sometimes he wants me to fuck him, too, but I don't get the sense that's his agenda tonight.

I pull myself up to sit beside him and take the v from between his fingers. While I drag from it, Wade plays with my soft penis, rolling it between his fingers. I could stiffen it in an instant, but Wade prefers for me not to, to let it harden on its own when I become genuinely aroused. It's a common request with clients—natural they'd want to feel wanted—which I usually ignore.

Wade leans forward to take me into his mouth. In a tick, I'll be hard too. I exhale my v and turn to the window. Still no mountains, only sky.

I can't stop thinking about Stone, about what's happening in Chiang's office, as I stand in her anteroom. I'm not supposed to feel sadness and, right now, I wish I couldn't; a tautness spreads through my chest, up my spine, to the back of my skull.

Dock stares at me like he's itching to ask me a question.

I pace to the huge window at the far end of the room. We're fifty stories up in Chiang's gaudy neon-and-glass high-rise, looming over all the shorter, surrounding towers. Below us, tiny gray dots mill around in their tiny gray lives. I think of how many I've ended. I've never thought to ask why Chiang needed me—and the rest of her army of Butchers—to murder so many people, a relentless stream of snuffed lights. Stone's death has me pensive. I need to snap out of this.

Dock shuffles up beside me. "Bull..."

I don't answer him or dignify his presence.

If I counted all the humans forming a lackluster kaleidoscope on the streets below, and counted all the holo-corpses on my tablet, which number would be higher?

Dock clears his throat. "I got drained today. First time."

"Good for you." I don't have any desire to discuss Dock's rite of passage with him.

But he touches my arm, a surprisingly gentle gesture for a Butcher. "Was it strange? Your first time?"

I turn to him. He's so young—though, for the most part, we all look the same age—and it occurs to me that due to his youth and his role as Chiang's errand droid, he may not yet have killed anyone. My first murder is imprinted in my memory stronger than any of the hundreds that have followed, more vivid than last night's kill.

I leaned against the cold wall, a red vaportube in my fist, and gazed up at the sky. Raindrops rushed to my face, exploding on my cheeks and forehead. Past them I could see the faint twinkling of a dozen stars. I didn't understand what any of it meant.

Chiang had told me my target would find me, that she'd arranged a meeting.

He showed up eventually with a warm, toothy smile, oblivious to his fate. I thought he was handsome, with a heavy brow protecting dark eyes. He approached me as if we were friends and, as the flickering fluorescent above me played on his features, I noted what looked like a Butcher-scar along his cheek, but on the wrong side.

Chiang had been very explicit in her instructions. Not on the street, she said.

I grasped the steel handle of the door beside me. "Let's get inside."

The mark slipped the vaportube from my hand as he passed me, pressing it to his lips. He turned back, still smiling, to exhale the v in my direction.

"No, Bull—"

The vaportube shattered at his feet, its slimy scarlet fluid spreading around our shoes.

I shot him in the abdomen. It was not a standard Butcher pistol, less powerful, but one Chiang loaned me special for this, my first assignment.

As his hands swung in to close around his spurting wound, I fired again.

Make it slow, Chiang had said. I knew not to ask why.

I perforated his torso five more times before he stumbled to his knees. He didn't beg. His final word—my name—still lingered around us like smoke. He gazed at me with an expression I didn't understand as I drove the gun's muzzle into his forehead.

His voice was ragged, weak, heartbroken. "Bull."

I squeezed the trigger.

"I don't want to talk to you, Dock." I move away from the window, back towards the door to Chiang's office.

"It's just..." He follows me across the room. "They say you're different. I—"

I spin around. "Yes. I *am* different. I'm the only Butcher who gets *angry*."

He nods, but after a moment of silence, speaks up again. "You don't need to, do you?"

I don't. I'm not sure how he would know that. Maybe he's defective, too.

"Butchers don't look out for one another, Dock. We're not *friends*." I wipe the lingering rain from my jacket sleeves. "But Stone helped me, when I came online, and he's being retired right now. While you're trying to talk to me about ejaculation."

The door opens. Chiang's bodyguard Judge—now the oldest Butcher I know, but of a different generation than Stone—fills the doorway, beckoning me inside.

Stone sits upright on the sofa at the far end of Chiang's spacious office. His face shows no expression—not that it ever really did—but his shirt's been removed and his chest carved open. Wires and synthetic organs crowd the space where his pro-core should be; it sits in his lap, a dulled metal box the size of a human heart.

"It's funny about you oversized tablets." Chiang faces away from me at the window behind her desk, a red vaportube balanced between her long fingers. Shiny black hair—tangled in a single braid—hangs to the middle of her back. "I could have transferred him to a new body, if I'd wanted."

Chiang draws on the v, then exhales her vapor against the window, temporarily blotting the sky and the city below. I settle into the wooden chair facing her desk. Judge hovers to the side of her desk, his amethyst eyes tracking my every movement.

"He didn't want that." I lean forward.

Her fingers tense like talons preparing to skewer prey. She turns to me. "Butchers don't *want* anything, Bull. If they did, I'd have a problem. Anyway, I thought about making him an Uttie, wouldn't that have been funny?"

Of course she knows about Stone's and my unusual relationship, and she's needling me because she can. I show no response.

Chiang is not a conventionally attractive woman. Her cheekbones are too high and her mud-colored eyes are too small, while her mouth is a bit too large. But men flock to her, can't get enough of her, drawn to her power. She enjoys picking up random men at trashy nightclubs, but always keeps at least two Butchers at her side. One is always Judge, but her whims decide who else she'll bring, and sometimes it's me. I hope that's not what she has planned for me tonight.

She wasn't always like this, I've heard. But the rumor is a Butcher murdered her husband while he was visiting a Doll. I don't really care about the gossip.

"So, Bull, I summoned you here this morning and... you're just showing up now?" Her v gurgles as she draws on it, filling the room with the scent of sweet berries.

"Butchers need sleep. It's a flaw in our design."

Chiang smiles, but I can tell she isn't amused. "Well you, in particular, are quite defective. So was that one. His excuse was he was old." She points to Stone then crosses around her desk to sit on its edge, directly in front of me. "I've wondered about you, Bull. Would you fuck me if I asked you to?"

This again. I don't know if she has a bad memory or if there's some meta-level to her asking me this a half-clock times now. "Of course."

She taps her vaportube on my head like I'm her pet. "Would you like it?"

"Probably not." This is true, but not for the reasons she might think.

Chiang laughs, a surprisingly soft, infectious giggle that jangles against every other aspect of her appearance and persona. "I wouldn't either. You aren't my type, for one."

She's told me this on plenty of occasions too. It's likely a lie. I know her type. She prefers lumbering brutes, the human equivalent of Butchers, and so the only way I miss that requirement is my status as a droid. I've accompanied her on clocks-worth of nights cruising for hookups, I've stood as her second bodyguard while these men—muscle-bound savages, usually—attempt to ignore the Butchers hovering over them enough to satisfy Chiang's insatiable sexual appetite. She likes to make them think she's so displeased—even when it isn't true—that she'll have them killed. On more than one occasion, she's made me drag a screaming naked man out of her bed, set him on his knees with my weapon shoved into his neck, while she pretends to dispense mercy.

"Anyway." Chiang crosses her legs, kicking my knee in the process. "I have a job for you. Good news is, you're not going to be chasing some schmuck all over creation. Bad news is, you'll need to be stealthy because this asshole is heavily guarded. It has to be you because all these other overgrown microwaves clomp around like fucking robots."

She reaches behind her and grabs a shiny metal square the size of a fingernail. I lean forward as she presses it into my forehead. Images beam into my op-procs, accompanied by scrolling white text.

Memories flash at me, too, but most evaporate like the exhalation from a v-tube before I'm able to grasp what I'm seeing. Foreign emotions flood my central cortex, and I jerk forward, knocking the naildrive to the floor.

Chiang shoves me back into my chair. "You really are a piece of junk, you know that? Pretty. But glitchy as shit."

"And not your type." For once, instead of struggling to form a smile, I have to fight to suppress one.

This catches her off-guard and she laughs—not her soft, sweet laugh but the other one, the bile-filled snort. "A mouthy Butcher. Lucky me. You get the files before you fucked the transfer?"

I push my chair back and stand. "Big play."

Chiang draws from her v but doesn't exhale. "Only kind worth making." She waves me out of the room.

On my way out, I steal a final glance at Stone. I didn't notice before: a hint of a smile lingering at the edges of his mouth.

This is my last kill.

six. MIX

I know Wade's routine by now, generally. Within a couple ticks of walking in my door, he's fucking me, and, a couple ticks after that, he's done. Then he likes to mess around a bit, but eventually nods off. He stays down for fifteen ticks max and then he's ready to go again.

While he's out, I get up and straighten my room. I set the lube bottle back on the nightstand and fish out clean hand towels for our next go, then collect the used towels and deposit them in the hamper hidden in my closet. I hang my robe on the edge of the privacy screen accordioned along the wall and fold Wade's clothes into a neat pile. Finally, I duck into my private bathroom to freshen up and, invariably, it's while I'm in the other room that Wade rouses.

"Hey, come back!" His voice pitches a bit too close to a whine for my liking, but I oblige.

Wade's already helped himself to the lube and worked himself back up to full size. It really is quite an impressive sight, and my cock begins to inflate as well. I grin. "I guess you decided what's next on the menu?"

"You, baby. It's always you." His oily fist makes a sloppy smacking sound as he slides it along his shaft.

"Hmm." I climb beside him and slip my fingers behind his head, pulling his lips to mine. I push my tongue into his mouth aggressively and when he whimpers, I pull away. "I thought we might flip the script a bit."

If it's too easy for him, he'll grow bored. The city teems with other Dolls, other options, some of whom he already owns.

"Oh, you wanna fuck me instead?" Wade's eyes darken a bit, his expression turning more serious as he considers this.

My hand slips between his legs, rubbing the inside of his thighs until my knuckles are tickling the fuzzy underside of his balls. "Maybe."

I don't. It's much easier to let him fuck me. My fully hard erection is much too big for him and getting it inside is a delicate and time-consuming process. Unlike me, he still experiences pain and squeals with every wrong move I make. Once he relaxes and lets me inside, I think he prefers it, to let someone take control, but it also challenges his masculinity. The only time he's ever gotten

27

rough with me is after I've shot a load inside him. Like he needs to prove who the alpha is.

"You'll go slow?" His eyes lighten as he warms to the idea.

I roll onto my stomach, craning my neck to kiss his neck as I shift my hand onto the base of his shiny, slick cock. "Of course. I know how you like it."

Wade reaches forward to grab a handful of my ass. "I might need to fuck you again first. I'm too worked up."

For a shrewd businessman, he's surprisingly easy to manipulate.

I let go of him and let my head fall to the pillow. Wade rolls onto me and, before I have the chance to inhale, he's thrusting away. He pins my arms and drives himself in and out of me with a frantic, manic energy—because I questioned his dominance for a moment—but it doesn't bother me. A tick later, he's slowed into a calmer rhythm.

The second fuck always takes much longer. I don't watch the clock, but it could be twenty, thirty ticks before he's ready to shoot again. While he grunts softly into my ear, I usually let my mind still, but tonight I'm distracted thinking about the future he's envisioning for us. He says he wants out of his current life, to get out of the city. He promises to get me out from under Chiang's thumb but is vague on the details. Does he imagine we'll live like lovers, like equals, in domestic bliss somewhere far from here? Or would I transfer to him as property, a plaything he could pimp out should he ever grow bored? He might be naive, but I'm not.

He rolls me onto my back and props my legs on his shoulders. "Mix?"

In the mirror leaning beside the privacy screen I can see his back, his muscled ass clenching as he enters me again. He might be offended if I ever admitted to him my opinion that his backside is his most attractive feature.

"Do you like me?" He caresses my temple, sliding three fingers around my cheekbone to pull my attention towards him.

He gets this way sometimes. "Of course. Not just your magnificent cock."

Wade maintains his rhythm—slow strokes in, faster strokes out—but his eyes darken. "It's not my cock I'm worried about."

I touch his cheek. "I really do."

Do I? As a client, he's a dream come true. As a person? I don't really know him.

That seems to satisfy him as he picks up the pace. "I've got... plans..." He keeps interrupting himself to grunt. "...for you... and me... oh fuck... oh fuck..."

Then it's over.

After the second orgasm, he always gets talkative. We sit shoulder-to-shoulder at the head of my bed, passing my vaportube back and forth. Wade reaches for my hand.

"I'm making a move soon. Real soon." He presses his sticky fingers against my knuckles. "Gonna get out of this place but... I don't feel good leaving you."

I glance towards the mirror but, from here, all I see is our feet. "What do you mean?"

Wade sighs. "I'm not an idiot, Mix."

I squeeze his hand. "I know—"

"You're a Doll. If I didn't have money, you wouldn't waste a tick on me." He drops my hand but rests his palm on my knee. "But I think you like me. I hope you do."

"I keep telling you—"

"It's just words, Mix. You're programmed to tell me what I want to hear *and* you know what I want to hear better than I do. Dolls are fucking *smart* and you're the sharpest one I've met." He massages my knee. "But... in spite of myself, I really fucking like you."

I don't know why, but hearing those words arouses me and my cock twitches. I'm not sure if Wade notices. "So what are you proposing?"

"Nothing yet. But promise me you'll think about it when it's time?"

"I always consider my options." I drag my palm across the soft fuzz on his chest. "Now what about that fuck you promised me?"

Wade laughs. "Let me close my eyes a minute first. You wear me out, you know?"

Well, that and the mild sedative I put in the lube he likes.

He slides down to lie on his back. I tuck my head into the crook of his neck and massage around his sternum, pressing my fingers into his pectoral muscles. He shifts to bury his face in the pillow, and I switch to rubbing around his shoulder blades until his breathing stutters. He'll be out for a few ticks.

I slip from the bed and creep to the clothes I folded earlier. I fish his mini-tablet from his pants pocket and carry it over to where he snores. A face-scan and a finger-read unlocks it.

I sneak into the bathroom where I've hidden a secret, second tablet underneath a stack of towels. With a few swipes on his device, I'm in his account. I set up an instant transfer of ten megachits to my unmarked, black market tablet. The money I siphon will be life-changing for me but is likely insignificant to him. Still, I suspect that he won't be pleased when he uncovers my duplicity. Though I've yet to see it, I know he's got enough of a temper and an ego to risk a turf war with Chiang over those stolen chits, should he ever notice the missing funds or the mysterious transactions. I don't intend for him to find out, not until it's too late.

He *is* buying my freedom, he just doesn't know it yet.

I gaze up at the run-down building, at the warm light spilling from a room on the top floor, five stories up. It's an old apartment building of weathered gray brick, taller than the shuttered shops lining the rest of the block. I don't come to this neighborhood if I can avoid it. Unlike the overpass where I sleep, the people here never seem to rest, always shoving and shouting at one another.

Someone's stolen a crate of food, and a desperate crowd scrabbles around them. *Please, I have babies*, I hear a woman shout. A gunshot echoes in the distance, followed by the whir of a siren. The crowd freezes for a beat and then resumes. A skinny, middle-aged man shoves me as he emerges from the throng, a chunk of bread dangling from his mouth. When he sees who I am—*what* I am—the bread drops and lands in a puddle at my feet. *So sorry, I didn't see you.* His fear excites me, causing my trigger finger to twitch, but I shake my head and push forward.

This is my last kill.

After that encounter, the crowd parts for me, as if they can smell my presence.

At the center of the disturbance, a teenage girl huddles over a metal box. She clutches half-loaves in both hands, frozen as she studies my approach, as if I won't be able to perceive her if she holds very still. Her eyes bulge as I lumber closer.

"We're so hungry." The girl's voice is soft, like a whisper, and sad. Her bony fingers tremble, digging into one of the loaves.

I glance away from her, towards the door of the apartment building. A Butcher named Pyre stands guard, thick arms crossed over his chest. He isn't one of Chiang's, but we've crossed paths before.

I lower myself to a crouch so my face is almost touching the girl's ear. "What's your name?"

She swallows, steeling herself. "Sarah."

"I'm not here for you, Sarah." I set my hand on the open crate. Peeking beneath the bread are bright red apples, and I think of the man I murdered last night. Or was it this morning? He was a thief, too, and I never asked what he had stolen. I touch Sarah's still-trembling hand. "Please be careful, though."

She stares at me. The acrid scent of her fear is gone, replaced by something else. Relief? Anger? I'm only programmed to respond to a single emotion.

The crowd lets me pass and, once I'm gone, returns to desperate shouting as if I was never there. I keep my eye on Pyre as I approach the building. When he turns his head away from me I leap to grasp the rusty fire escape ladder. Peeling paint scrapes my palms as I lever myself up, and the ladder creaks noisily, but Pyre doesn't seem to hear.

Once I've scaled the ladder, I'm certain Pyre won't see me; I'm a creeping shadow on a dilapidated wall. I scan the still-shoving crowd and the rest of the rainy street for other Butchers, but it seems I'm in the clear. Still, I keep my body low as I ascend the rickety metal stairs to the top of the building, darting quickly past every lit window.

The one I need to enter is unlocked, but stuck. I peer inside. An ornate privacy screen blocks the view of half the room. On the other side, I see a bed that fills most of the space. A naked man sleeps face-down. I can't tell if it's my mark, and I'm a bit concerned because I was expecting two occupants—my human target and the droid who lives here—though I've only been tasked with terminating the human. I avoid killing non-targets whenever possible.

I jiggle the window until it unsticks then force it open, crawling into the room that smells of incense and sweat and droidsex. I hear nothing except faint snoring, another muffled siren in the distance, and receding footsteps in the hall.

This is my last kill.

I never think past the last-kill part. What would I do instead?

The maybe-target stirs, as if dreaming, driving his face into an oversized pillow. That alone makes me think this *is* my target—the missing second occupant is a droid—but I creep around the bed anyway. Each step is cautious, deliberate, as the wooden floor is likely to creak with a misplaced footfall. Once I'm able to get a better look at the sleeping man, I grow more convinced he's who I'm here to kill, but I won't fire without seeing his face. Other Butchers shoot first and ask questions later but this is a delicate job.

Once I'm all the way around the bed, dangerously close to the door, I unclip my weapon.

His head pops up, eyes open. It's him. Kevin Wade.

"Wait, you're—" Wade raises a hand to stop me.

I yank the pillow from the bed and shove it into his face, knocking him back down onto the mattress, while my other hand grasps my weapon. I press its muzzle against the pillow and fire.

Feathers swirl around my face.

This was my last kill.

I'm swatting them away when I hear a voice behind me.

"What the *fuck?*"

I aim my weapon in the direction of the voice. I presume it's Mix, the Doll who works in this room, but the sight of him flusters me in a way I'm unaccustomed to. I don't know where he appeared from, but I've been caught unawares before. No, that's not what's throwing me off.

Dolls are attractive by design, but my breath catches at the sight of this perfect model standing naked before me. Emotions rumble through my chest like storm clouds, settling low, between my legs.

Mix doesn't flinch, appearing more infuriated than frightened, shifting his glare from me to Wade's corpse. "Get that thing out of my face, you fucking savage."

I've aimed this weapon in hundreds of faces. Never have I encountered someone so unruffled; even ice-hearted Butchers usually beg for their lives. I lower the gun and put my finger to my lips. Wade has Butchers posted outside the door and they won't hesitate to blast us both into component parts if they catch wind of what I've done.

"Fist and Stab?" Mix shoves past me, gesticulating angrily towards the door. "I don't give a fuck about them *or* you. Breaking into *my* room, killing my whale. Fuck you, Butcher."

He yanks the ruined pillow from Wade's body and hurls it toward me. More feathers float through the room like a confusing snow. I stare through the flurry at him. His eyes are a cloudless sky, floating above his sturdy jaw and narrow, expressive lips. I tear my gaze away long enough to pull out my tablet.

"I need a holo." My voice sounds like it's emerging from somewhere behind me, like I'm speaking in my own ear.

Mix shoves me with surprising strength and I stumble backwards, slipping on the pillowcase on the floor. "I don't care what you need. You have no fucking clue what you've done."

I raise my tablet and snap the holo anyway. Wade's face is barely recognizable—charred synthetic feathers stuck to the fragments of his skull that peek through the gunshot wound—but it's good enough. I turn to Mix. Not a whiff of fear. "You're not scared of me?"

Mix snorts. "You? Get the fuck out." He points towards the window.

As I work myself back out to the fire escape, I hear him again, speaking to the droids in the hall. "Your boss is dead, so either you're free now or you can go kill the Butcher who just climbed out the window."

I don't glance back but peer over the edge of the fire escape. Five stories. I'm sturdy enough to handle a leap from this distance, so I swing my legs over the edge and let myself drop. Gunshots ring out behind me.

eight. MIX

I've never cried before—though I can—and I'm not going to start tonight. But I wish I was emotionless like Fist as we both study the corpse of his former employer. No, owner. Wade always referred to his droids as his employees but it's a euphemism. Droids are property.

It doesn't matter. Wade is dead. My luck's run out.

"What now?" I carry Wade's clothes over to his body, sneaking his mini tablet back into his pants pocket. Whoever orchestrated this hit—my money is firmly on Chiang—will want that, and I do not need that sort of heat.

Fist looks at me, blank-eyed and slack-jawed. His normal Butcher-implacability is reading to me as stupidity now. "Has this ever happened to you before?"

"No, I've never had one of you shitheels sneak into my room while I was in the bathroom and murder my client." I gesture to Wade's legs, hoping Fist will get the message that I want him to lift them up so I can get Wade back into his clothes, but he refuses to take the hint.

"What were you doing in there, anyway?" Fist's expression doesn't waver, but I have to acknowledge he's possibly smarter than he looks. Droids don't need bathrooms like humans do. Even when we consume their food. I'm not really sure where it goes but I think we might incinerate it.

I tug Wade's pants over one of his calves. He isn't even cold yet. "Freshening up. So what happens to you now? Are you a free agent or something?"

Fist finally figures out what I'm doing and levers up Wade's other leg for me. "If Chiang did this, she'll take over our contracts. I'll probably be fine, but Tire and Pyre—"

I stifle a laugh, out of respect to Wade. "Your friend's name is Tire?" I liked Stab better.

"He's not my friend." Fist seems to notice Wade's penis for the first time and pokes it cautiously like he thinks it's playing dead.

"Those two are older, and this was their detail. They fucked up. Chiang might retire them. I hope they're not still chasing her Butcher. If they kill him, they're as good as scrap."

"Did you say you *hope*?"

Fist continues toying with Wade's dick, pinching it, like he's forgotten all about helping me. "Butchers are a lot more complicated than you think, Doll."

"Sure. Quit molesting the corpse and sit him up, please?" I'm not even sure why I'm so fixated on dressing Wade. He's dead. He doesn't care if his cock is out now. But for some reason, I do.

You wear me out, you know?

As I finish buttoning Wade's shirt, a Butcher stomps into the room. I think it's Tire—I still prefer Stab—but it's so difficult to tell a lot of Butchers apart.

"Get him?" I step back to survey the crime scene my room has become and sigh.

"I was wondering when you'd realize that was a suicide mission." Fist finishes tugging on Wade's clothes for me.

Tire steps further into the room, eyeing me suspiciously. "Might not be a bad idea to punch a hole in Chiang's org. Make a vacancy."

Fist shakes his head. "This was a big job. Chiang must trust that one, whoever he was."

"He was handsome." I glance around, looking for my vaportube. It's on the nightstand; not worth navigating through the bickering Butchers to grab it. "Like they forgot Butchers are supposed to be hideous."

"Oh, I've seen that one around." Fist nods in my direction. "No, killing Chiang's golden boy? Might as well open up your own chest cavity and pluck out your pro-core. Definitely suicide."

"So that's why you stayed back." Tire crowds my personal space, towering over me. "You. How did this happen?"

I weave past him to retrieve my vaportube from the nightstand. "Wade got sloppy. Didn't bring his best crew, obviously. And as much as I appreciated not having you ghouls around, he should have had one of you stationed here. He used to do that." I point at Fist.

Tire moves into my space again. "You should watch your mouth, Doll."

I exhale vapor into his face. "Or what? You going to endear yourself to your new boss by killing her best Doll?"

"You're not special." Tire pushes past me to my window, glaring out as if he's going to spot the assassin still crouched on the fire escape. "You're a droid, same as me."

I could tell him that we're not the same. I make people happy, and he makes them dead. But it hardly seems worth it. Tire turns away from the window and shoves past me again with unnecessary force. He scoops Wade off the bed like the dead man weighs no more than my ruined pillow.

Fist stays behind a moment. "Did you like him?"

"Wade?" I shrug, tracing the starburst of blood on my sheet with my eyes. "He paid very well and treated me better than he needed to. So yeah. I guess I did."

"I don't know what that's like." Fist follows my gaze to my ruined linens. When Wade first started hiring me, Fist was the one he'd bring into the room with us. He'd stand facing the wall, all night if he had to, never allowed to turn around. "He wasn't good to us."

I draw on my v. All I taste is bitter now. I sink onto the mattress. "I'm sorry."

"He put this thing in me... I can feel some pain." He sits beside me. "But not much else."

I offer him my v, but he declines. "You've been coming here for years and I don't know your name."

He holds up his malfunctioning hand. "Everyone calls me Fist."

I shouldn't laugh, but I can't help it. "I feel like we're having a moment, Fist, after all this time. I could give you a free—"

Fist shakes his head. "It hurts. Everything down there hurts." He stands, reminding me how massive he is as he runs his finger in Wade's drying blood on my sheet. "He wasn't good to me at all. But thank you."

I finally realize what Fist is trying to tell me, and an unusual sensation roils my innards. If I had human food inside me, I think I'd vomit.

"Hold on." I clamber over the bed, scattering feathers everywhere, and fish a card from a stack in the bottom drawer on my nightstand. I hand the card to Fist. "This guy might be able to help. I get all my tech from him."

Fist accepts the card and studies it like he doesn't understand what's happening. Then he turns his gaze to me. "We're not what you think we are, you know."

Before I can respond, he clomps out of the room, rattling the empty vase on my nightstand.

I don't want to be left alone with my thoughts, so I jump up the moment he's gone and yank the destroyed linens off my bed, wrapping them around the sad remains of my favorite pillow. I'll take them to the unhousement camp on the other side of town, where someone will be glad for a bit of extra warmth or comfort and won't mind the blood stains. Along the way, I'm certain I'll run into a john or two, hungry men willing to toss me a handful of chits. Losing Wade is a setback, but I'm not giving up. I'll find a replacement whale. It's what I'm programmed for. In the meantime, I need to stuff down my pride and work the streets, same as I used to.

As I'm sweeping up as many of the feathers I can catch, Jemmi raps on my doorjamb. "What the fuck happened here?"

I frown. "Butcher broke in and assassinated my whale."

She swoops in to smother me in an embrace. The strap of her nightgown slips, and one of her nipples grazes my abdomen. I like Jemmi but I sometimes wonder if she's trying to play me the way we play our clients. It's a flaw in our design: so we could adapt to our human clients' intricate needs, they made us much too smart. But she doesn't know I was scamming Wade, so there's really no angle in this for her.

I gently pull away. "I'm going to go out and get rid of this mess and get used to slumming it again."

"Oh, Mix." She tucks her errant breast back into place and her expression brightens. "Want company? I could use some more air... and a chit or two."

I retreat to my closet and select an outfit without really thinking about it. Something cute to attract men's eyes, but not too fancy since the rain's picked up again. "You're a love. But I'd like a minute to clear my head."

She glances at my naked bed. "Did you... did it...?"

"No." I dress quickly. On the top shelf of my closet, I have spare linens, which I pull down. "I was in the washroom."

Jemmi helps me make up the bed as if nothing happened, then walks me to the front door, kissing my cheek and wishing me good luck.

Outside, the rain is relentless; it's another miserable night. The noisy crowd from earlier has dispersed, leaving a large, empty crate in the middle of the street. A bloated loaf of bread, half-eaten, floats in a puddle. A woman perches on the steps of a condemned building, sucking on an empty vaportube and tracking my steps with her eyes. I can feel her judgment from across the street.

A skinny, greasy-haired blond man beckons me into an alley. He offers me a single chit to ejaculate in my mouth, fishing a pencil-thin erection out of his torn pants, and calls me uppity when I decline.

I know I'm in a better neighborhood when the potential johns call to me from their portos, not from across the street, and when they roll down their windows to reveal chubby cheeked leers, cocks poking from beneath rolls of middle-aged belly fat. One guy wants to fuck me but instead I give him what the other guy wanted for fifty times the price, still clutching my bloody package like a hungry child. After he cums, the man asks me where I'm heading but doesn't offer me a ride.

Back on the street, I pull up the hood on my sweatshirt. It's a miserable night.

Frigid rain batters the dead Butcher's face. Pyre. He might not really be dead, since my gutshot likely didn't damage his pro-core and definitely didn't touch his central processor. Maybe he could be rebooted and returned to service, but I doubt anyone will bother. Chiang's rival Wade—who I just killed—was legendary for doing fucked-up mods to his droids. I've seen it in action. I once saw Pyre harassing a Doll for a draining, demanding to penetrate her. Butchers aren't supposed to have any desire for that, which is why they need drainings in the first place. I pulled him off before he managed to hurt her, but I'm sure he went and found some other Doll that was either desperate or foolish enough to let him have his way. I prefer not to picture what likely happened next.

So I don't feel bad about putting this one down. He's only the second Butcher I've ever killed.

This was my last kill.

Tonight's rain makes last night's seem like a warm shower in comparison, but now that I no longer have a vengeful Butcher trailing me all over town, I can finally get back to my tent and find warmth. I've already sent Chiang the holos of my kill in the brothel so, hopefully, I won't need to see her for a few days.

I pull my jacket tighter around my chest but it does nothing to slow the invading chill. The icy rainwater seeps through all my clothes and my skin prickles, raising goosebumps. I don't understand why we were created with such specific, useless human vulnerabilities. Was it just laziness that prevented our designers from crafting entirely new beings? They built us exactly like them but selectively omitted key components. Those choice omissions allow our owners to subjugate us, but they left in so many unnecessary inconveniences. Goosebumps are one. Or why Butchers need regular drainings.

A porto pulls up beside me, its back window whirring as the passenger rolls it down. "Hey, how much for a throatie?"

I continue walking, but turn to face the human attempting to flag me down. His unremarkable face flushes red once he sees my scar, and his panic is so powerful I can taste its metal on my tongue. My finger twitches. The window rolls up and the porto speeds away, spitting its fumes in my face.

As I approach the overpass, I pass a sunken-cheeked woman whose dull ash-colored hair hangs over her eyes as she pushes a rickety trolley overflowing with other people's discarded trinkets. She flashes a near-toothless grin when she sees me. "Evening, Bull!"

I'm surprised she knows my name—I don't know hers—but I've definitely seen her around. The longtime residents of the unhoused village are much friendlier than the crowd of desperate scrabblers I encountered earlier outside the brothel. Those people might be lacking sufficient food, but they mostly have homes to return to. Here the humans band together in a shared resignation.

At least once a week, someone doesn't wake when morning arrives. They carry the body to the center of the village, and everyone gathers around. If anyone knew the deceased, that person might say a few words of remembrance. Then the body is burned, and everyone soaks up the temporary warmth. I usually stay inside. It's a human ritual; not for me.

"Have you seen Quentin today?" I attempt to reciprocate her smile but I need more practice.

She shakes her head, exposing large brown eyes, and leans in conspiratorially. "Kill anyone interesting tonight?" A powerful scent of urine wafts off of her, but unlike humans who are repulsed by the odor, I find it comforting.

I see no harm in being honest. "Kevin Wade."

Her already oversized eyes grow even wider. "Oooh. You're one of Chiang's then." She gazes past me and wipes more hair from her face. "Why do you slum it with us?"

This time the smile works, appearing as an involuntary response. "I'm defective."

"Aren't we all?" She laughs then starts to maneuver her cart away from me. One of the wheels wobbles and whines. "Have a good night, Bull."

I should have asked for her name. Chatting with her for a minute allowed me to momentarily forget the bitter chill, the shiver beginning to convulse my limbs, but once I'm alone, those unpleasant sensations dominate my consciousness.

The moment I spot my tent, I realize something's wrong. A shadow moves across its length, cast from the inside. Instinctively, I unclip my weapon as I march towards it.

I'm able to see inside once I get close enough. A young couple—both no older than twenty human cycles—crowd my heater on the edge of the mattress. The girl sees me approaching and clamps a hand over her mouth to stifle a scream. The boy doesn't offer as violent a reaction but his obvious, paralyzing fear smells sweet, fruity and powerful. My fingers curl around the butt of my weapon as I climb inside.

"What do you want?" The girl's voice is defiant, like she's ready to die for this lodging.

I'm about to assure her that no one needs to die, but that this is *my* tent, when I see the dog sitting beside the man. Her scruffy fur is a mottled brown, and she studies me with trusting, hopeful eyes. A neon-colored lizard stuffy hangs from her mouth. Her tail wags, thudding against the threadbare floor of the tent.

I release my weapon and reclip it. "This is my tent."

"We found it." The girl glares at me with red-ringed, emerald eyes and grasps the boy's hand. He won't face me, shaggy blond hair tumbling over his face. They both look reasonably well-fed, with rounded cheeks.

I turn my attention back to the dog. Once again, she wags her tail.

"I know." I dip my head and duck out of the tent.

I sit in the stain where Quentin's ragged tent should be, but the ambient warmth from my heater isn't enough to counteract the absence of any rain protection. A shiver snakes up my spine and electrifies my limbs. I stand.

The shiver abates as I walk, but I'm exhausted—I'm unaccustomed to running for my life—and the longer I walk, the more my legs hurt from the massive fall I took earlier to escape the brothel. All the rain-protected areas under the overpass are already lined with tents.

A beautiful female Doll catches up to me. "Hey, Butcher, what's your name?"

"Bull." I glance in her direction—blue eyes, matching colored hair held in pigtails—and accelerate my pace. I know what she's going to ask.

"You're awful handsome for a Butcher." She struggles to keep my pace in her impossibly tall heels. A ridiculous human invention. "I'm Holli. Need any help tonight?"

"I'm good, thanks." Then I pause. "Who do you work for, Holli? Wade?"

She steps closer. I smell a man's desperate sweat on her. "You gonna tell me he's dead? Let me get out my party hat. You think I should run? Some of us enjoy what we do. I could show you—"

She reaches for my crotch but I gently intercept her wrist and push her hand away. She nods and walks away in the opposite direction without another word.

I continue my trek to the far side of the encampment. People sit outside the rain-protected tents, but everyone's too tired or hungry to be afraid of me. Some nod in recognition. Once I reach the end of the encampment, I circle around the perimeter on the far side, where the city peters on the brink of a gang-infested wasteland.

My legs hum with an unfamiliar ache, and walking no longer keeps the shivers at bay. I pass a parked porto with its door hanging open. Inside, Holli spots me and waves from underneath a red-headed man with a muscular ass as he jackhammers her. I wave back, grateful that she found someone to increase her evening take.

Back at the cityside border of the encampment, I notice a large dead tree. Its barren branches might provide a bit of relief from the rain, so I settle in beside it, decaying bark scratching the back of my head. I pull my sore knees to my chin and try to control the shivering. Once my teeth start chattering, I know there's not much use.

It's going to be a very long night.

ten. MIX

I t's truly miserable. I don't get out after dark that often, but I can't remember the last time it's rained this relentlessly, like every drop carries a vendetta against me and my ultramarine outfit. It feels apocalyptic.

The usual sidewalk johns have all retreated inside, taking their easy handie-chits with them. A porto eases in beside me but when the window lowers, the man inside looks so unhinged—and I swear I see blood on the seat beside him—that I tell him no.

"You can't say no!" He hurls his door open, smacking me in the hip.

Pleasure oozes from the impact point like a deep-tissue massage, but I cry out anyway. It's better if I don't let on about my mods.

"Fucking whore. You have to do what I ask." He charges at me like one of those machines they use to demolish the tenements in my neighborhood. I think he might tackle me, but he stops an arm's length away to collect his breath. He stands in a puddle that devours his shoes. "I'll make it worth your while."

I give him a once-over. He's average height for a human male, not muscular but big, probably much stronger than he looks with a significant weight advantage. A wispy mustache flutters like a caravan of lost insects above his chapped lips.

"All right, calm down. What's on the menu tonight?" I tap the middle finger of my right hand into my palm. Then the fourth finger twice, and the middle finger again. It's the code for the second most-expensive tech I have illegally installed. An emergency self-defense mechanism.

I shoot my arm out to the wannabe-john's chest and fire a powerful electrical current into him. It's enough to put a human down for a tick or two but will barely slow a Butcher. The man convulses and drops to the pavement. Normally I'd take the opportunity to run. But I can't tell if he's conscious, and the puddle he crashes into is so deep he could drown.

Maybe he would have killed me, but I'm no murderer. I set the bag containing my linens and pillow on top of his porto and drag him to safety. Once I realize I've gotten him halfway there, I continue on carting him across the street, finally hoisting him up and back into his porto. He's definitely

45

unconscious, but his stuttered breathing assures me he's alive. I snatch my donation bag and sprint off before he rouses.

My arm aches from the electrical burst. It's a type of pain my other implant doesn't handle, so it actually hurts. I don't mind. It was absolutely worth it to witness his stunned expression as the electricity surged into him. Motherfucker thinks he can just order any Doll to do his bidding. He'll think twice the next time.

I haven't felt pain, or not much, for the majority of my lifecycles, since my implant blocks most of it. It's not a sensation I ever expected to miss. But now I'm reminded: the pain assures me I'm alive.

I slow again after a few blocks, grateful that I wore sensible shoes.

As I approach the sad encampment where all the unhoused humans cluster, a blue-haired Doll approaches me. I recognize her face, but only because she shares it with Lida, a savvy operator who works out of my house. Sometimes I wonder if there's another Doll—or even some other model—out there wearing the same face as me, but I feel like I'd have heard about him by now. That sort of laziness wasn't in fashion at my incept, as our unique designs were considered a selling point. The earliest Butchers—the oldest of the droid families—were mostly identical, though not many of them are around anymore.

We aren't manufactured with planned obsolescence as a design feature anymore. When Chiang's predecessor got murdered because his trusty old bodyguard Butcher glitched out at precisely the wrong moment, she spearheaded a movement to make sure we lasted longer so that wouldn't happen to her. I'm grateful, I suppose. At ten cycles—twelve if I'm being honest—I'd be on the scrap heap by now if she hadn't done that. But I'm pretty sure I don't want to be sucking cock for chits sixty cycles from now.

"Hey, you work for Chiang, right? I'm Holli." The Doll trails slightly behind me when I don't slow down to chat. She reeks of human body odor and probably doesn't even know it. "How is she to work for?"

I roll my eyes. I'm not in the mood for political upheaval. "She's not going to win any humanitarian awards. Was Wade as bad as they say?"

"Not to me. He wasn't so rough with the girls."

First rule of business, handsome. Don't cum where you eat. Too messy.

I wish I hadn't asked. "Chiang's a fucking monster, but she mostly leaves her Dolls alone. If you get into a good house, you can work your way up to having your own room. She sure as shit isn't raping anyone, but she's tough. She doesn't like a suck-up. If you get a face-to-face, show her why you'd be an asset."

"Thanks... I didn't get your name."

I know what's coming. "Mix."

She slows, as if we aren't moving through torrential rain. "You're the one—"

"The one and only." I pause before another small lake of a puddle and turn to her. "Don't take this the wrong way, love, but you should go home and change. A john's covered you in his stink, and it's going to turn off other tricks."

I continue on and, this time, she doesn't follow. I suspected I'd picked up something of a legendary status among Wade's droids, especially now that I know he wasn't exactly benevolent—and definitely not gentle—with them. Let them talk, I think. Let them wonder about me.

On the outskirts of the encampment, I spot the most pathetic, shivering creature curled up against a tree. Exactly the sort who might benefit from two bloodstained sheets and a leaking pillow. The warmth of my benevolence spreads through me.

Until I see his face.

His eyes are closed and his teeth chatter wildly. I've never seen a Butcher react to the cold this way. They don't feel pain or discomfort, or aren't supposed to. When I used to work the streets and would regularly have to drain them, I'd sometimes punch or squeeze their testicles and claim it was a routine part of the draining, just to amuse myself with their complete lack of reaction.

I stand over him as the rain floods from his stubbly scalp across his face. He's actually quite handsome when he isn't pointing a gun at me.

"Well, if it isn't my least favorite Butcher." I may have learned enough about Wade's terrors not to mourn him, but I can still mourn my access to his chits.

The Butcher opens his eyes. Recognition registers on his face but he doesn't speak, averting his gaze away from me.

I pull the pillow from my bag, scattering feathers on the ground, and toss it towards him. "Remember this? Thought I'd donate to the needy. Truly didn't expect that to be you." The pillow strikes him in the knees and settles at his feet.

He doesn't look up. "Leave me alone."

Next I pull out the linens and throw them at him as well. One catches on his leg and drags over his calves while the other settles on top of the pillow. "Ever sleep in the blood of your victims?"

47

The Butcher pulls his legs tighter to his face.

I fish my v from my pocket and draw on it. The sharp sweetness tingles on my tongue. "I have to say, I never thought I'd see a Butcher shiver. Chiang won't pay to lodge you?"

He shakes his head, slow. I flash to a memory: the surprised expression on his face when I emerged from the washroom. I saw something in his eyes I didn't fully register at the time, stunned and angry as I was. Was it... regret?

I glance down at the sheet on the ground. Wade's previously dried blood leaches into a puddle. "Typical. You got a name, handsome?"

"Bull." His deep voice quivers from the cold.

He might be a savage murdering Butcher. He might have ruined my night and my best shot at escape. But his violent response to the cold intrigues and excites me, like a mystery for me to solve. He's not bad to look at, either. And I can't stand to see him shaking like this.

"C'mon." I extend a hand, and find I'm surprised when he accepts it.

eleven. BULL

A few Dolls—some male, mostly female—lounge in the foyer in identical see-through robes. All eyes turn to me as we enter, studying me warily. A powerful scent of mildew hangs in the dimly lit, wood-paneled room, and I immediately think coming back here was a mistake. But my drenched clothes weigh me down, all my limbs ache from the violent shivering, and my teeth are still chattering. I can't pass up the opportunity for shelter.

On the stairs, we pass a Doll who shares a face with the girl I met in the unhoused encampment—Holli, was it?—though this one has purple hair, not blue, and no pigtails. She flashes Mix a flinty smile.

Mix's room seems smaller, more cluttered than I remembered. The only evidence of the murder is a smattering of feathers—some bloodied—drifting across the floor.

Mix sweeps his arm dramatically, gesturing for me to enter. "Excuse the mess. Some idiot destroyed my best pillow." He follows me in and immediately slips off his coat, which he tosses towards a chair on the back side of the small space. It misses and lands on the floor, but Mix doesn't seem to care. "Take your clothes off. You'll shave off a whole life-cycle with that shivering, and I don't need you warping my floors."

I hug my arms around my chest though it doesn't provide any additional warmth. I'm completely out of my element here. I've never even visited a Doll for a draining. "I can't—"

Mix rolls his eyes. "Damn right you can't afford me. Get naked, you muscled lug."

I stare at him, paralyzed.

"You're killing me, Butcher. At least take that horrible jacket off." Mix unbuttons his shirt and slips it off, his well-defined physique glistening with rainwater. He drapes the shirt over his privacy screen and retrieves a towel from his closet. He blots the wetness from his chest and spiky black hair.

I manage to get my jacket off—I've carted human corpses that weighed less—and set it on the chair in the corner, but then I find myself back in a standoff with Mix, my arms crossed over my chest again. Still shivering.

He eyes me warily, a hint of mischief in his eyes. "Butchers aren't shy."

49

"I am." I wipe water from my brow. "Can you turn around at least?"

Mix draws off his vaportube, its sugary scent filling the space between us. "Absolutely not. You're not going behind that screen, either. *Never turn your back on a Butcher.* Everyone knows that." He sighs. "Let me help you."

My eyes widen in panic, and my already weary muscles tense, but I don't say no.

He closes the distance between us and sets his soft fingers against the prickled skin of my exposed forearm. "Put your arms down. I'm not going to hurt you."

I do as he says, feeling as vulnerable as if I was already naked. "I don't think you could."

"You'd be surprised." Mix presses a gentle finger over my pro-core. "Now I know you're not new. I'm guessing you're about my age. So you must have been with a Doll before."

I don't answer, but I suspect my silence tells him more than any words I might have said.

"Interesting." He runs the finger across my chest, pausing to release the top button of my shirt, then slides it downward until it falls away. Sparks fire along my spine. No one's ever touched me with tenderness before, and I find strange sensations radiating from the base of my skull. His gentle touch finds my wrist again. "Can you close your eyes for a tick?"

I definitely should not trust a Doll I've just met—who very well may have a vendetta against me for murdering his client in his bed—but I don't have much choice. It's Mix's room, and this time I'm here by his invitation. His rules. Aside from that, I do trust him, even if I shouldn't.

In darkness, I hear the gurgle as Mix draws from his v once more, followed by a soft exhalation. The sweet vapor seeps into my skull as Mix's tender fingers work their way down my chest and abdomen. I feel a rush of warmer air against my skin as he spreads my shirt open and the rough fabric of his towel as he dabs away the rain. The floor creaks softly beneath his feet as he crosses around me, tugging the shirt down my arms from behind. His breath is at my neck as his arms circle my waist.

"Wait." I open my eyes, facing the window I crawled in earlier. Raindrops streak the pane in a hypnotic pattern. Mix steps into view, his summery eyes an even richer blue than I'd remembered. "Why are you being kind to me?"

"Sometimes a boy wants a monster in his bed?" Mix shrugs with a dramatic hand flourish, darting his eyes towards the mattress. "I don't know."

I suspect he does know, but isn't ready to tell me yet. He kicks off his shoes and unbuttons his pants, then slides the wet fabric down his legs with the grace of a dancer. The storm clouds I felt tearing through my chest before return with increased ferocity, and my gaze keeps darting to Mix's plump, dangling penis. I barely noticed it when I was here earlier, transfixed instead by his bright blue eyes.

I unclip my weapon and set it on the floor beside the bed. "I appreciate the hospitality but... I don't understand what's happening right now. I told you I can't afford you."

His eyes flick towards my pants, and I know he sees the outline of my thickening erection. But he shakes his head. "Nothing is happening, Bull. I've offered you a warm bed, that's all. Have you ever slept in a bed?"

"I sleep on a mattress in a tent. But squatters took it." My hands converge over my crotch, only drawing more attention to what's happening there. I attempt to flood my head with other images, hoping to stem the shame of revealing the throbbing contents of my pants, but my focus keeps returning to Mix. His soft fingers, unburdened by physical labor or the business of death, tracing my sternum. The patience and kindness peeking beneath his arch façade.

Mix tuts like he doesn't believe me, then turns to the window. "Fine."

I quickly pull off my boots and pants. I don't know where to put them, so I leave them in a heap on the floor. When I glance up, I notice there's a mirror against the wall. Mix's reflection flashes a mischievous grin—he's likely seen everything. I forgot how crafty Dolls are. My face burns red with embarrassment.

That's never happened before, but all of this is unfamiliar. I've never experienced an unintended erection before either.

I dive for the bed and pull a navy-colored sheet over my waist. The ones I ruined were a paler, purpler blue. As soon as I'm covered, Mix slides into place beside me. He sucks on his vaportube and offers it to me.

"No, thank you." I shake my head. "Hey. I'm sorry for earlier. You were... attached to Wade?"

Mix sighs, filling the air with fruity vapor. "I thought so, a little."

He sounds wistful. I resist the temptation to apologize again, reflecting on how I'm in unmarked territory now. The scene earlier—Mix's rage at discovering Wade's murder—is one I've experienced many, many times. I've felt a woman's fists pounding on my chest after I'd just blasted off her husband's head, and I've seen the petrified eyes of children I'd orphaned. The immediate anger is familiar.

Discussing it later is entirely new.

Mix continues. "He wasn't a kingpin to me. Once he became my regular, my biggest whale, it was easy to pretend he was just some lonely, wealthy human. But..." In my peripheral vision, he shakes his head. "Turns out he was just another terror."

I cock my head and look at Mix, but eye contact makes me uncomfortable so I return to gazing at my knees. I'm acclimating to the warmth, and my erection has receded some, but this is all still so strange. I imagine this is what humans mean when they describe something as *dreamlike.* "You did say you wanted a monster in your bed. But you really didn't know?"

I thought everyone knew what Wade did to his droids, particularly the male ones. Chiang certainly did; she included it in the dossier she downloaded into my brain earlier.

"I didn't need to." Mix shudders with a rueful laugh. "He was my ticket out of here."

When Mix offers me the v again, I accept it. I've never tried it before. "Maybe I did you a favor. He wanted to buy you from Chiang?"

The vapor smells better than it tastes. The flavor is artificial and cloying, barely masking the bite of epi.

"Yes and no." Mix rests his palm on my knee—its warmth radiates up my thigh—and leans in so close his lips graze my ear. "I was stealing from him."

I'm overcome with more unfamiliar sensations. The unexpected physical contact causes my erection to return with such force that it's impossible to ignore it stirring the sheet like the awakening of a slumbering sea beast, but that's not the sensation that surprises me the most.

I feel *protective* of Mix, this canny and mysterious droid I've just met, suddenly nervous at the imagined repercussions if Wade were to ever uncover this duplicity. Someone may still review the dead man's finances and piece it together.

Mix doesn't seem concerned. "But that's the past, and the past is boring. Am I wrong that you want to kiss me?"

Butchers don't want anything, Bull.

But I do. My hand flies up and seizes the back of Mix's neck—he still isn't afraid—so I can pull his face close, close enough for our mouths to touch. I shouldn't know how to do this, but I do, and I feel like I'm short-circuiting—all the wires in my head and chest and groin feel like they're flying loose inside me, firing sparks in every direction—as my curious tongue pushes past his lips. He smells of citrus and rain.

Mix grasps the sides of my skull and gently eases our faces apart. He grins. "I thought so."

Despite initiating the kiss, Bull looks as surprised by it as I am; his eyes are wide and childlike, not the expression of a hardened killer at all. It's all new for me too. I've never kissed a Butcher, or met one who could get hard without assistance.

"Let's not rush anything." I let go of his head.

Bull blushes again, dropping his chin and casting his eyes downward. "You're right. I should go to sleep. It's been a long fucking night." He sucks on the v, though I can tell he doesn't like it.

"I'm sorry." I study his body. Butchers are usually massive, with barrel chests and thick necks, descendants of the earliest models who were little more than murderous tin cans. Bull is different. He's a bit shorter, though he still towers over the average human. But that's not what catches my attention. What I find unusual is how well-defined his physique is, not just large like the standard Butcher. I want to ask him about it, but now isn't the time.

Bull shakes his head. He stares at my knees, hidden under the sheet. When he speaks, it's barely audible. "It's okay."

I slip my finger under his chin and raise his gaze to meet mine. "You don't know what I'm apologizing for, Bull."

A Butcher once told me that they are programmed to react to fear, that it triggers a response in them. They can smell it like dogs. Dolls are the same way but with desire, and Bull wants something from me so bad it makes me salivate.

He's waiting for me to answer my own question, but I take a moment to assess his face. His eyes are dark, darker than any I've ever seen, like two black holes plunked in the middle of his face. Most Butchers have odd-colored eyes—the one I drained this morning had bright purple irises—to better provoke an unsettled response from humans. They're intentionally ugly, with mismatched features, but Bull doesn't have any of that. I wonder who designed him and how Chiang got a hold of him.

"I'm sorry for siccing Wade's Butchers on you before." We make eye contact for a moment—before Bull shifts his gaze over my shoulder—and I see a roiling tornado of suppressed emotions. Interesting. "I was furious but also, I had to. I needed them to see you or they'd pin Wade's murder on me."

Something resembling a smile flickers across his face like a shooting star. "I figured. We're all just trying to survive."

"And you shook them, obviously."

"Not quite." He sighs and runs his finger along the vaportube. "Every time I kill someone—even other droids—I promise myself it'll be the last one. I've broken that promise a thousand times, but I keep making it." He keeps his voice soft. It tickles the back of my skull.

I feel an unusual hum near my pro-core, like something that doesn't belong has found its way in there. At first I imagine swarming insects, but the more I focus on it the more I picture the iridescent wings of dragonflies.

Bull keeps talking, his timbre barely above a guilty mumble. "Chiang says I'm defective."

I grab his thick shoulder and squeeze. "You're not defective, Bull. You're just not... you're not what they say you are." I intentionally echo Fist's words to me: *we're not what you think we are.* But I mean something else.

I haven't quite figured it out, but I know I'm close. It's been nagging me since the moment I found him in my room, hovering like a ghost over Wade's fresh corpse. Something I saw when he swung that gun into my face.

"What am I then?" He finally lifts his chin to look at me. He looks lost, and I think I need to tread lightly. If I push him in the wrong direction, his confusion could reshape itself into anger.

I sometimes feel like I'm the only one who's figured out that Butchers are the most harmless creatures in the city, with a few exceptions, because they don't experience anger. But I've established Bull is different, and I have no idea what he's capable of. "Can I ask you a very personal question?"

Bull nods.

"What do you think about when you drain yourself?" I brace myself for an explosive reaction but, on some instinctual level, I know Bull enough to know that that's not how he'll respond.

What I get is surprise. "How did you know—?"

I point to his crotch. "Butchers don't get hard by themselves. If they could, they wouldn't need to hire Dolls."

Bull accepts this and gazes towards the window. "I imagine I'm somewhere else, where I don't have to kill anymore. I have someone with me. I used to imagine it was Stone—he was an old-school Butcher—but he got retired.

Sometimes it's Quentin, a human. But usually it's someone else. I can't see their face."

Dragonflies.

"I've had the same fantasy. Mine usually gets sexual. Sometimes when I'm fucking a john—or he's fucking me—I imagine we're somewhere else. It's someone else. I don't know who." I run my finger along the ragged topography of Bull's scar.

Iridescent wings.

Bull frowns. "I don't let myself think about that. You know why we're all male? So they can also use us to degrade people for their petty revenges. They put it in our programming."

The dragonflies aren't inside me anymore; they've become me, and I flutter outside of myself. I lean forward and kiss Bull, wrapping my arms around his back. I pull him down on top of me.

He probes my teeth with his tongue, and I think for someone who has never done this before, he knows what he's doing—

I know what needs to happen next.

While Bull continues to kiss me, his restless hands exploring my body, I swing my legs around his back to drive his body closer to mine and use my hands to press our faces even closer together. His pro-core whirs against my chest, and I see butterflies with intricate stained glass wings. They flap their stunning sails, slow and shy; the room fills with them. The sound of their flight is music, and I am lost in it, humming my iridescent appendages through it.

Bull pushes off of me, then sits up. "What are you doing?"

For once in my life, I am speechless. I want to tell Bull that I'm feeling things—seeing things— that I've never experienced before, but my tongue betrays me. I stare at his beautiful, serious face, unable to decide if I've provoked anger or if he's just confused.

Or sad.

"I can't. You know I can't."

I try to pull him back down to me again, but he's too strong and too stubborn. Aptly named. I find my voice. "But do you want to?"

Bull shuts his eyes for a subtick, his chest expanding as he inhales. On exhale, his eyes open, and he gazes down at me. I recognize his expression, and it's the only answer I need. He chokes out a word anyway. "Desperately."

I yank him down and, this time, he lets me, his sudden weight against my chest knocking away my breath. My fingers run down his spine; one charts a course around his side and between his legs. An uncontrollable whimper burbles out of him, and I realize it's coming from me too. I fill my lungs with air. "Trust me."

Bull presses his lips to mine while I reach further. I find his erection. My touch follows a vein, tracing it upwards. Bull moans. I take hold of him and set him in position and—

I'm a dragonfly, and I lift higher, my wings a forgotten song.

"Oh...wow..." Bull looks stunned. He holds himself perfectly still, his shadowy eyes rolling away to reveal white.

I'm a dragonfly, humming in my own ear.

"You won't hurt me." My voice rises from outside my body, appearing as a whisper.

Bull moves slowly at first, the shocked expression he wears telling me he's savoring every subtick. He keeps gazing down at me like he can't grasp what's happening, as if repeatedly asking *is it supposed to feel this good?* without ever moving his mouth.

I pull him tighter. Once he's drawn all the way back and slid all the way inside again, he builds up speed. The ecstasy is almost too much for me, but it isn't converted pain. It's the shared hum of our pro-cores, two beautiful wings beating against the night sky.

His confidence blossoms with every stroke. He pushes onto his forearms, never letting me free of the gravitational pull of his mesmerizing eyes, and he *smiles* at me. Before I have the chance to acknowledge that I've never seen a Butcher smile before, I find myself laughing, at the absurdity of all this, at his impossible beauty.

Outside, the rain beats against my window, washing away the world. There's only Bull and me. It's more than I can take, but I don't ever want this moment to stop.

Then it does.

thirteen. BULL

I don't love the man I'm fucking, but he loves me. Love is the opposite of my programming; it's for humans and their weak, failing bodies. I press the butt of my hand into his throat as I drive myself into him over and over. He grasps my wrist but doesn't try to pull it away, driving nails into my bone. The pain makes me fuck him harder. I don't love him and never will, but I do like him.

When I tell him I'm going to shoot, he begs me not to. More. He always wants more.

I pull my hand from his neck and stroke his cheek, my affection fueling his passion ever more. He's a handsome man, with eyes like shadows lurking beneath a strong brow, and I enjoy the way he stares up at me like he's seeing God. A thin scar snakes along his left cheek, curving towards his eye.

He reaches towards my face—

"Bull?" Mix grabs my chin.

I glance around. Mix's room, same as it was before, with the never-ending rain assaulting the window. I shake my head. "Something's wrong."

He moves his hand to my chest, above my pro-core. "You're not overheating."

"It's not that." I—

I—

I put my hand over his. He tells me what a beautiful body I have. I flash a shy smile, like I haven't heard this a hundred times before, like it's not really a compliment to whoever created me. I met him at my incept. He was so pleased with himself, anxious to try me out.

The man I'm fucking wouldn't know any of that. He only knows about buying things he wants. I like him, but I could never love him. Even if I knew how. I try to say his name, but I don't remember what it is. Something's wrong.

I tell him again I'm about to cum and cover his mouth before he can tell me no. Paul, that's his name. His eyes plead with me. He loves me. He's told me as much. I don't think he knows a thing about love either. He's got a wife and meets me in secret.

I hold off. He's fun to tease.

He pulls me in like he wants me to kiss—

No—

"Bull, what's happening?" Mix taps my cheek. When I fail to answer right away, he pushes me off him, once again surprising me with his strength.

I'm feeling something else I've never experienced. Overwhelmed. I stare at the dull yellowed ceiling and press my palm to my pro-core. Mix is right; I'm not overheating. But everything feels out of place, a puzzle constructed out of mismatched pieces. "Chiang might be right. Maybe I *am* defective."

Mix props himself up on his elbow to face me. His presence is comforting, like an old friend, not that I have any real idea what having a friend feels like. I turn to him and find his expression is *concerned*. No one's ever cared what happened to me before, except Stone, and only in his very limited Butcher way.

"Was it the fucking? Was it too much?" Mix finds my hand, slipping his fingers between mine. "Talk to me."

I close my eyes, and in the darkness, I see Paul again.

I lifted my weapon—not mine, someone else's—and waited for him to turn. The smile died, and his fear rankled my nostrils.

"No, Bull—"

I fired into his stomach, a red flower blooming in its place. He rushed to close the wound, but I fired again. And again. And again.

"No. I went somewhere else." I pull myself to a seated position, my back against the wall. A shiver creeps through my extremities, spreading like disease. "I was in a different room, fucking someone else. But—"

Mix joins me at the head of the bed, clasping my hand once more. I expect him to ask me how I could have been fucking another person when he's my first, but he doesn't. "Who were you fucking?"

"His name was Paul." Mix's face is too much for me, too beautiful, too worried. I want to go to sleep and not-dream but, instead, I turn to the window. The rain has slowed, and I think I see a sliver of moon, though maybe I'm imagining it. Maybe I just want it. "I killed him, later. But—"

Mix takes my chin into his soft hand once more, tilting my face towards his. He kisses me, not the sexual kissing of before, but something else I've never felt before: sweetness.

"I knew something wasn't right about you, the moment I saw you." He pulls a blanket over us, and I didn't realize how cold I was until the soft cotton touched my skin. "You're smaller than most Butchers and the only one I've ever met—and I've met *plenty*—that I would call handsome. But when you spun that gun at me, Bull, I saw *sadness* in your eyes."

"Chiang says I'm a failed experiment." I sigh. "They were trying something different, but I'm defective."

Mix shakes his head. He reaches for the vaportube that's rolled to the middle of the bed, but once it's in his hand he doesn't use it. "None of that is true. I've been trying to figure it out since I found you outside—"

"Is that why you brought me here?" I become hyper-aware of my nakedness, even though the sheet covers me to my waist, and wish I had dry clothes so I could leave. Everything I've seen and felt from Mix has been a lie, more Doll-machinations. He's probably planning to use me against Chiang somehow.

"No." Mix squeezes my hand and barks out a low laugh. "You looked beyond pathetic, shivering out there. I watch out for our kind, even Butchers."

"Never trust a Doll." I pull my hand away. "I want to go to sleep."

Mix looks genuinely hurt, but I don't believe it. Something else swirls in his eyes. I don't understand it and don't care to.

"Everything that's happened tonight has been genuine. I felt sorry for you, so I brought you here. Then I discovered you're not at all what I expected." Mix reaches for me again but stops before his fingers can find my skin. "Or what you think you are."

"What the fuck am I then?" I pull the sheet off—I don't even care that I'm naked and cold—and clamber out of the bed. I can't stay here anymore. Dolls don't know how to do anything but manipulate, and I should have known better. I grab my shirt—still sopping wet—from the privacy screen and hold it over my nakedness. "What am I, Mix?"

Mix stares at me. Through me. He opens his mouth.

"A Doll."

The word echoes in my head like a gunshot down a lonely street. I try to open my mouth to protest, but words fail me. I can't move. Time seems to stop. My shirt drips onto my toes.

"You've been over-programmed, Bull." Mix leans forward, concern creasing the corners of his eyes. "It's the only answer that makes sense."

A sparking circuit of realization fires at the base of my skull: he may be right. All these *feelings* I've struggled against my whole life as if they were bugs in my code were never accidents at all. All the killing I've done. But I resist. "That can't be."

Mix pulls away the sheet covering him. "It's why you feel things other Butchers don't. How you can remember something that couldn't have happened." He inches towards the edge of the bed, cautiously, like a sudden movement might startle me. "Please don't leave, Bull."

Chiang knew. Every time she flicked her eyes after calling me a heap of junk, it wasn't because she prized me as some secret weapon. She was lying to me. Every time she called me defective, she knew the truth of what she'd done. "But... why?"

"I don't have the answer to that." Mix stands. He pries the shirt from my unmoving fingers and pulls me towards the bed again. My feet follow him. At the edge of the mattress, he strokes my cheek, my neck.

Everything is upside-down, and the colors are all too bright. Every tiny sound ricochets inside my skull, but when Mix touches me, I feel *safe*. He kisses my ear. I don't want to leave anymore. I've felt this safety, on some level, since he first extended that hand to me in the rain.

Mix pulls me onto the bed. It feels warmer than when I left it.

"It's not just you." He pulls the sheet up to our waists again, then traces the length of my abdominals with a single finger. "I experienced things tonight I've never felt before."

I try to hold onto that feeling of safety. "When I was inside you, I saw what I always do. But you were with me, Mix."

"I saw dragonflies." He rests his head against my neck, continuing to caress my stomach. "That's never happened before."

"Never?" I put my hand over his.

"After thousands of men. I didn't think I could feel anything new. Intimacy's always been a transaction. That's my core programming. But the dragonflies were beautiful." He puts his lips to my cheek. "I'd like to see them again."

I see a sunny hill dotted with swaying flowers, a tiny cabin in the distance. I feel Mix's hand in mine, his fingers soft as a whisper, fingers that have never gripped a gun. I see us at a table, sharing fruit, because there's no one to tell us not to, and it tastes good. I see myself waking in an old wooden bed to find his arm around me, his pro-core humming at my back.

BUTCHER THE DOLL

I climb on top of him and feel the future beckon.

fourteen. MIX

I thought I'd wake this morning with Wade beside me. Instead, I find Bull, sitting up and watching over me. He looks different in the morning light, his features softer. He smiles when he sees me open my eyes, then his hand rushes to his mouth, feeling its edges like he's not sure he's doing it right. I could get used to waking up to this view.

"I killed your v." He reaches into his lap and hands me the spent vaportube. "Sorry."

I hoist myself to a seated position. Bull tilts forward to peck my cheek then retreats, embarrassed. I'm still hearing the wings of dragonflies. "You don't even like it."

For my next tube selection, I grab a yellow and catch myself thinking: I hope Bull likes this one better.

"It's an acquired taste." He rubs his knee against mine. "I couldn't sleep. My brain refused to cycle down."

I draw on the yellow v. It's sour, and my lips pucker. I don't think Bull's going to be a fan, yet I hand it to him anyway. "I'm not surprised. Your whole identity's been upended."

Bull twirls the vaportube between his fingers. "In a way, but no. I'm still a Butcher. I still work for Chiang. As long as she doesn't send me to kill you, I don't see how this changes anything."

"Except you know how to fuck now." I grab for his dick, and he doesn't stop me. It stiffens in my hand and mine follows suit.

"True. That v's not going back in the tube." He reaches for my cock—which he hadn't done before—and I'm definitely not complaining. "What do you have lined up for today?"

"I was hoping you'd stay a while."

He shakes his head and releases my erection. "I can't. I never checked in with Chiang after last night's job. She'll probably have some new bullshit assignment for me." He finally draws from the vaportube and looks like he actually enjoys it. "I'm definitely going to have to kill someone."

"And I'll probably have to fuck a half-clock of guys before the day's over. We have our programming, right?" I glance over at the window. The rain appears to

65

have finally stopped, but the morning sky is a charcoal gray with no sign of the sun anywhere.

He looks at me, suddenly very serious. "This is real, right?"

Iridescent.

"I think so." I take the v from him but, this time, I'm the one fiddling with the tube rather than drawing from it. "Have you ever thought about running away?"

Bull nods. "Every day. But I don't know if there's anything else out there. And Chiang's never going to let either of us go. She'll mobilize every Butcher she has—and now she's got twice as many, with Wade gone—before we ever see a hillside."

"I like that you said *we*."

Bull smiles. He's getting better at it. "That was the other thing. Maybe the main thing for me, that I didn't know what I'd do outside the city. My whole life, or at least the one I remember, has been going from kill to kill. I couldn't imagine what else there was for me."

"My plan wasn't to run. I've seen that fail too many times." I suck on the vaportube, rolling its amorphous contents on my tongue. It's sweeter this time, less sour, and less bitter than the other flavors. "I asked around what the market value is for a Doll my age, and I was siphoning money from Wade to buy myself out."

"So Chiang fucked that up last night." Bull stretches. Seeing him change position reminds me how impressive his physique is. I've never seen a Doll as bulky as he is, so I wonder if they rebuilt him to better resemble a Butcher. "But I think she's going to regret it."

I grin. "So should we fuck again before you go?"

Bull throws me onto my back—after seeing his sensitive side, I find it easy to forget that he *is* a Butcher, and incredibly strong—and pushes his tongue into my mouth. I flash to the stranger in my room who'd just assassinated my whale, to the shivering silhouette in the driving rain, to the strange Butcher who was too shy to take his shirt off in front of me. It hasn't even been half a day.

I wonder if the change in me is even greater. I can't grasp what's come over me, but I don't want to ever stop feeling this way. I haven't been overprogrammed to become something I wasn't supposed to be. I've just uncovered code in my programming, an entire universe of new emotions.

Bull sits up. "No. Not now. I'll come back after."

He's right. It'll only get harder to separate. It's just strange for me because I've never *wanted* anyone before last night. Wade was right. If he'd come to me broke, I'd have told him, politely, to fuck off. But Bull? I wouldn't accept his chits even if he had any. This is new. "That's probably best. You will come back, right?"

He grins—really working those facial muscles like a pro now—and strides naked to the privacy screen. "I promise."

I stand as well, to head off the discovery he's about to make: his clothes are nowhere near dry yet. In my closet, I find him a pair of pants that were always too baggy for me and a shirt with enough stretch that it might fit across his massive chest.

He frowns. "I'm not ungrateful but... do you have anything else... less colorful?"

I slip my arms around his waist from behind. "Or you could stay here until *your* clothes are dry."

"You know I can't." But he pulls me even closer. "How about a compromise?"

I laugh, certain he can feel my suddenly hard penis throbbing against his leg. "What changed your mind?"

He turns and lifts me off my feet with seemingly no effort at all, and I'm not small. Physical strength has never turned me on before—in my line of work, it's more of a threat than any sort of bonus—but I've only seen Bull use his gently. That's the turn on.

I know Bull's already lied to me once this morning, but he's doing it to protect me. I'd do the same for him. I'm trying not to think about it.

He hoists me onto the bed, lowering me to the mattress like a prized possession, and rolls me onto my stomach. This is new for him too. My body thrums with anticipation.

"This okay?" His low voice tickles my ear.

I nod.

The room erupts with dragonflies, a riot of iridescence, a shimmering hum. I imagine I'm grasping at the large insects, as if I could touch them, as if I could capture something so magnificent. I want to harness the moment in all its fleeting glory, the feeling of Bull on top of me, his gravity driving the air from my lungs, and the sensation of him inside me, a puzzle piece gently snapping into place.

He grunts into my neck, guttural and deep, and I feel his muscles tightening against my back. I think: I've tamed a monster.

And a monster tamed me.

Once we're finished, I laugh. "If you'd stayed a Doll, you would have put me out of business."

Bull manages a grin before rolling off me to face the ceiling once more. I wish I had my tablet nearby, my holo camera, so I could record these moments.

I might not see him again.

I feel like a different person as I leave the brothel in Mix's tight, multicolored pants and shiny, form-fitting shirt. I'm not, though. Nothing has changed.

Except the rain. It finally stopped sometime during the night. A weak sun struggles to burst through the clouds, a circle of brightness like a bleach stain on the muted ash of the sky. It feels symbolic, but it isn't. Nothing has changed. Not yet.

My first stop is my old home. When I see Quentin, I no longer need to question the stirring in my chest. It's relief. It's happiness.

"Bring me any meat, Mr. Butcherman?" He flashes his wild, off-kilter grin. "I see there's new people next door. You renting the place out?"

I settle in beside him. "Something like that. I was worried about you yesterday."

The opening to my old tent is unzipped, and the pup peers out. She disappears and then pops her head through the opening again, this time with her green stuffy. I smile.

Quentin pats my shoulder. "You never need to worry about old Q." He squeezes my shoulder, grabbing a fistful of my uncharacteristically bright shirt. "Looks like you got it all figured out now."

A heavy transpo rumbles on the roadway above us.

I turn to Quentin, my breath catching in my throat. "You knew?"

His smile wavers, the edges of his mouth trembling. "I knew the old Bull, yeah. Wouldn't say we were friends. You helped me out once when you didn't need to." He pats my arm playfully. "Naw, not like that, we never did nothin' together, but you were always kind to me. Old Q don't forget his debts. When I saw they put that scar on your face... I been looking out for you since."

"All this time, Quentin?" Another transpo rolls above us like muted thunder—the increased traffic likely due to the better weather—and showers fine concrete debris at our feet.

Quentin nods. "Didn't see how knowin' would help you."

I close my eyes and don't want to open them again. Someone nudges my arm and when I look, I discover it's not a person; it's the pup. She drops her toy in my lap.

The man in my tent appears at the opening, his fear pungent and sharp, but my finger doesn't twitch. Maybe I *have* changed.

"Nala, come here. Now!" His voice is thin and desperate.

I give Nala back her stuffy and raise my arms. "I'm not going to hurt her. Or you. The tent's yours." I stand and scratch Nala's head. Her tail wobbles wildly. "Take care of it. Someone important to me bought that for me. And look after old Quentin here."

The man looks shocked but his fear dissipates in a soft breeze. I shake Quentin's hand, then I stride past his tent.

"I like the new look!" Quentin calls after me.

The city pulses with life, as everyone wants to get outside on the first clear days we've had in ages. Scents I'd almost forgotten drift through the air: fresh-roasted coffee, a street vendor reheating rolls. Everyone is happy and no one is afraid of me.

I meander to my destination, basking in the city's overnight transformation, charting the sun's progress burning through the heavy clouds. Shirtless men laugh as they play a game in the middle of the street. Dolls lean against walls, waving at me as I pass. Spring nips at winter's heels. Even without sunshine, it's a beautiful day.

I run into Dock outside of Chiang's building. He's in his shirtsleeves—I don't think I've ever seen him without his gray nylon jacket—exposing bulbous forearms beneath biceps that look like they're about to burst out of his skin. "Just the droid I was coming out to find. Saved me a trip."

I pat him on the back and he glares at me, surprised. One of the few reactions Butchers can easily show, and Dock displays it more than most, in part because he's so young but also perhaps it's just part of his personality. I wonder why they let us have that one. I don't know, but I'm sure it's nothing good. "Hey. You wanted to ask me something yesterday?"

It isn't easy to fluster a Butcher, but I think I've succeeded. He continues to stare, speechless.

"I know what I said. But maybe Butchers *can* be friends." I touch two fingers to his arm and, when he doesn't pull away, grasp its underside with my thumb. His skin is cool against my fingertips. "Maybe *we* could be."

Dock swivels his oversized head away from me in a gesture reminiscent of a petulant human child. "Quit fucking with me, Bull. I don't—"

70

"I'm not." I release his forearm and push his shoulder hard enough that he's forced to face me again, though he doesn't meet my gaze, tilting his chin towards the pavement. "You got a question? I'm listening."

His violet eyes deepen, revealing more blue than red. "Are you really defective? I feel things I'm not supposed to."

"You're not defective—"

Dock darts his head around, as if checking to make sure no one's listening to us. The humans drifting past us on the sidewalk seem too self-absorbed to bother. "Yesterday, I was nervous. I'm not supposed to be nervous, right?"

I nod. I still don't know what nervous feels like, but I suspect if I did, I'd be feeling it right now. "We're not programmed to, no, but—"

He interrupts me like he wants to spit this out before he loses his nerve. "I had my first draining and I... I liked how it felt. All of it. I thought—"

I put my hand to his chest to stop him, his pro-core buzzing against my palm. "There's nothing wrong with you. It's Chiang and everyone like her. They left all these emotions in our programming and use them to manipulate us. It's not enough for them to own us." I love my hand to his shoulder. "Let's get upstairs before Chiang gets impatient."

We start to walk. Dock turns to me once we're in the elevator. "Did something happen to you last night?"

I nod. "I figured out we need to look out for each other because the humans won't."

The elevator door opens.

Judge is waiting for us. He never speaks, and I wonder if Chiang stole his voice synthesizer. I wouldn't put it past her. Rather than ushering us into her office as usual, he leads us down a long hall to a smaller room where Chiang lounges under a UV lamp in a neoprene bikini.

She lifts her eye protectors as we enter. "What are you *wearing*?"

I cross my arms. "Why am I here, Chiang? I trust you got the holos."

She pulls off her goggles and sits up, waving to Dock to shut off the lamp. "Oh, you got somewhere better to be, Bull? Maybe I just wanted to make sure you were still in my employ. Wade put god-knows-what shit in his bodyguards."

"I'm fine. Had to end one of them, but I figured you probably would retire most of his Butchers anyway. It's his Dolls you want." I pace to the far side of the room. Judge never takes his eyes off me, and I notice he has his weapon unclipped.

"You're a smart one." Her eyes shoot to the left—her tell—before she approaches me and pokes my chin. "Nobody likes a smart Butcher."

I glance at Dock. "With Wade gone, it'd be chaos if anyone got to you too. The biggest players gone cold, all these droids with no owners? I hope you're stepping up security."

Chiang throws up her hands and shakes her head. Her ponytail swings wildly behind her. "Oh, you're angling for a promotion? Tired of sleeping in your little tent?"

"You know I'm smarter than the average Butcher." I step closer, towering over her. She smells of coconuts and greed. "And you know why."

Judge sets his hand on his weapon.

"Oh." Chiang's laugh is bitter and cruel. "Guess Wade's mouth was as big as his legendary cock. You're not gonna tell me you pieced this together on your own?"

Dock looks confused. Next to him, Judge looks ready to blast me into oblivion. That's his usual stance but, today, he seems more ready than usual.

"It doesn't matter. I'm still a Butcher, still yours. The only thing I remember is your husband was in love with me. Or thought he was. It makes sense why you'd use me to kill him." I step back and lean against the wall, between two terrible, incongruous paintings of flowers.

"Fucking Paul. Thinking I wouldn't find out he was planning to sneak off with one of Wade's Dolls. I could have just ordered one of his bodyguards to do it, of course. But where's the poetry in that?" She cackles again, crossing around the lounge chair to gaze out the window. "You weren't cheap, either. Wade had big plans for you. Pretty funny I used you to kill him, right?"

I catch eyes with Dock again, and he nods as if he understands. "Very funny, yes."

I'm not known for my sense of humor.

Despite the lie I've lived a thousand times, I've always known who my last kill should be, even before I knew Chiang had turned me into this monster. With Wade gone, she's the only obstacle blocking Mix's freedom, or so many others of his kind. Of my kind.

I reach for my weapon a final time.

sixteen. MIX

When the sun finally peeks through the cloud cover, casting my room in a surreal afternoon glow, I let myself accept that Bull isn't coming back. It's fine, I tell myself. I only met him last night.

I open my window, first to let the breeze circulate through my stuffy room, to let his heavy, woodsy scent dissipate into forgetfulness, but then I find myself crawling outside. The metal fire escape is still slick from the recent rains, though drier patches have begun to form, and I grasp for the cool railing. The sourness of my yellow v reminds me of Bull again, how he cocked his head like a dog the first time its flavor touched his tongue, how I thought he'd frown and thrust the tube back at me but instead his mouth shaped into a curious smile.

His smile, cautious like a whisper.

I shake my head to snap myself out of it and remember Sea rhapsodizing about Skye before their tragic grasp for freedom. I thought it was foolishness, and narcissism, since Sea and Skye were the same model and only a finger's width of cosmetic differences allowed the rest of us to tell them apart.

Now I find I'm jealous, despite their fate, that they got to live in the same house and spend so much time in each other's presence.

This isn't me.

I gaze down at the people on the street below. It's the first appearance of the sun in... I'm not even sure how long. All the shouting and discord has evaporated like the shrinking puddles lining the uneven pavement, as if everyone's forgotten their hunger, as if the still-weak sun could pass for sustenance.

The man who offered me a chit for a throatie last night stands in the same spot as before. He sees me on what I'm now imagining is a widow's walk, smiles and waves, as if we're friends. As if he wasn't spewing curse words at me half a day ago.

I draw on my vaportube and approach the railing like a monarch about to address his subjects. I wonder if working would take my mind off Bull.

A clattering inside shatters my reverie. I crouch to stare in my window and find Jemmi in my room, peering around, looking everywhere but at me. "Out here, love."

She rushes towards me so quickly, she stumbles over the corner of my rug. Like a cat, she continues on as if nothing has happened. "Mix! Haven't you heard?"

I don't need her to tell me the news—I can't even hear her when she tells me. My vision goes bright, washing her excited face in watercolors, then dim as she recedes into a bubbling lake of blackness. Her lips move but make no sound; all I hear is the distant, echoing laughter of unseen children, no longer joyous. Mocking me.

I'm definitely going to have to kill someone.

I could have stopped him. Could I? I knew, and I let him go anyway.

Jemmi is still talking.

"—a bunch of us are running... hey, Mix, are you listening?"

I hoist myself through the open window as Jemmi backs towards my bed to allow me into my room. "I fritzed a moment. Start over. Chiang's dead?"

Jemmi nods, gleeful. I notice she's wearing an oversized sweater and leggings, not her usual half-open robe. "One of her Butchers killed her. We're running now before someone can claim us."

The way Jemmi says *one of her Butchers* stings me, but I don't show it. "Who's we?"

"Pretty much everyone, Mix. You'd be insane to stay. Hurry up and pack." She rushes to my closet and fishes out the suitcase I lived out of before I had this room. "Word's out now so we don't have long."

I stare at the battered suitcase, a relic from a life I barely remember. Will this life, this room, the city feel that way for me in a few years?

If Bull's alive, the only place he'll know to find me is here. This room.

Jemmi's already throwing clothes in the luggage, grabbing items at random, yanking them from hangers. I'm touched that she's doing this for me, but she's doing it all wrong, pulling the wrong clothes. I stop her. "Which way are you going? To the mountains?"

She nods, her eyes watering. She knows I'm not going.

I'm surprised by her concern—I feel bad for questioning her—and pull her into an embrace. "Go, love. Don't wait for me."

Jemmi pulls away and stares at me in disbelief. "What's wrong with you? We were just talking about this yesterday!"

74

BUTCHER THE DOLL

I work up a smile, and a playful wink. "You know me, sweet Jemmi. I have my own plans. Now go."

Once she's gone, I return to the fire escape. A few ticks later, the exodus begins. I count them at first but after a clock's worth, I grow bored. I watch as Doll after Doll streams out of our house, our sanctuary, some with bags stuffed full of clothes, others with whatever's on their backs. Two unfamiliar Butchers accompany them.

This might be the stupidest thing I've ever done.

A tiny ember of cruel hope flickers inside me, and while it burns, I'll stay. I don't think there's as much of a rush as Jemmi and the others seem to believe. Chiang and Wade were the biggest players in town, and their competitors lack the Butcher-power to seize all, or even most of us.

I suspect I know how it'll go. They'll grab the more docile droids and reprogram Sous into Butchers and Utties into Dolls. Once the new Dolls have earned them enough income, they'll build more and everything will return to the way it was. I don't know the names of the minor players, but I suspect I might soon.

I climb inside and enter the hall. Gone is the everpresent sound of humans and their animal grunts, the squeals and moans of Dolls pretending to enjoy whatever's happening, pretending we're not imagining how we'll spend the tiny cut of the chits we're earning. The creak of the wood floor remains, the blood and semen stains on the stairs. The breeze from my open window pushes away all the perfumes and the sweat and the human desperation. The mildew lingers, flat and oppressive.

It feels like a new beginning, but I know better.

I settle on the front stoop and pull out my vaportube. The sourness tingles the inside of my mouth and feels appropriate as I exhale the vapor that temporarily cancels out the world.

A large, familiar figure rounds the corner, and my pro-core hums at the size of him before I realize it's not who I want. Just a standard Butcher.

He limps towards me and, as he grows closer, I recognize him. Dock.

I wonder if he was the one who did it, protecting his master, and my fingers tighten into fists. My nails dig into my forever-soft palms.

I punch in my self-defense code. I don't even care if he was the one. I'm certain he was there, and that's enough for me. It doesn't matter if he won't

75

feel it. I bought a strength upgrade years back and maybe I can further fuck up his crooked face before he yanks me off him. Rage churns inside me, a new, unfamiliar emotion, a tempest to rival last night's rains.

He points at me and stops. He turns and retreats, as if he knows I've entered my code and intend to pummel him with everything I have. I'm tempted to shout. *That's right, coward. Run.* But it feels silly. The rage doesn't fade but burns brighter, singeing the only available target: me.

Everything I've done since my incept was in the service of a solitary goal. My freedom. Now it's been offered to me, free of charge, and I'm hesitating. For what? A shy, sweet Butcher? A fucking idiot with a death wish?

I bury my head in my hands.

No. This is stupid. I'm going to return upstairs and grab what I need. I don't require any of my fancy Doll outfits, just a couple things, nothing sentimental—and, of course, my secret tablet. I don't know how much good it'll do me, but I worked way too hard for it to leave it behind.

I lift my gaze and see Dock approaching again.

He's not alone.

My pro-core hums so loud it deafens me. Dragonflies fill the air.

Bull.

He looks terrible: pale, spattered in human blood and droid fluid, his shirt—my shirt—torn and stained. He limps worse than Dock, leaning on the larger Butcher for support. He is the most beautiful thing I've ever seen.

Tears streak my face as I fumble to deactivate my self-defense code. I launch myself from the stoop, through puddles and street trash to get to him.

"I told you I'd come back." Bull lifts his head to smile—brighter than the sunniest day in memory—then groans from the expended energy. He coughs. "I promised."

Before I even reach them, I've formulated a plan. They're both too battered to run. I'll bring them inside. I doubt the escaping Dolls will have raided all the repair kits and spare fluid in their rush for the hills, so I can fix them up. We can run tomorrow, maybe the next day.

I resist the urge for a dramatic reunion kiss and position myself on Bull's unsupported side. I rest his oversized arm over my shoulder. There's no weight to it at all, like he's made of nothing but air. His hand drapes over my chest and it feels like the future.

"You're an idiot."

Bull laughs, his body softly convulsing beside me, and it's the most perfect sound I've ever heard. The sun warms our backs as we make our way back inside. The mountains will still be there tomorrow.

Acknowledgements

This story began as an entry in the Writing Battle competition, run by Max Bjork, for the Winter Flash 2024 contest. My prompts were to write an *Enemies to Lovers* story featuring the character of an *assassin* and the object of a *doll*. I was stuck at first as I tried to figure out how to make that combination work in a compelling way in one thousand words. My friend Alyssa Beatty jokingly suggested I write about the relationship between one character and a doll, which I seriously considered for a moment. Then another friend, Caio Rosario, teased me for my propensity to write about *sad gay robots* and the two concepts slammed together in my head and instantly transformed into this: what if the doll was a character? I owe another debt to Tracy Bradford for suggesting the word *butcher* when I got stuck thinking of a unique and memorable word for assassin droids. It's hard to imagine this story without that word now.

I originally wrote the flash version with a dual POV between Bull and Mix but I decided it didn't work, not at that length, so I stripped Mix's sections out and focused on Bull. I already had the idea to return Mix's POV into the story once I no longer had a word limit.

After I finished and submitted and was eventually allowed to share my original flash-length version of this with the wonderfully supportive Writing Battle community, many fellow writers encouraged me to expand this. I don't know how many were serious, but here we are.

First thanks to Jay Scott and Rachel Harbaugh for encouraging me to continue after I'd only completed two chapters.

Thanks also to Rachel Harbaugh (again) who jumped on the chance to be my first reader once I'd completed the novella version and assured me that I had not made a terrible mistake.

I don't think it's possible for me to list everyone who read the original story in a beta capacity, but I can try: Linda Bayley, Alyssa Beatty, Tracy Bradford, David Contara, Natalie Darnell, Erin Brandt Filliter, Christy Hartman, Trina High, April Ihly, Indigo LaRue, Aggie Novak, Avery Other, April Raines, Caio Rosario, Jo Spicer, Charlie Winter, and Mizuki Yamamoto.

CHARLIE ROGERS

Next up are the readers for this novella: Alyssa Beatty, Elizabeth Hakken Candido, Justin Creps, Katie Ess, Jaime Gill, Rachel Harbaugh, Haley Hwang, Melanie Mulrooney, MM Schreier, Lisa Short, and Jessica Wilcox.

A huge thanks to all my readers. I couldn't have done this without you.

I have to acknowledge the wonderful crew at Write Around the Block, and the slightly more unruly gang at the 1159 Discord server.

A few not-so-random shoutouts:

Talia Camozzi, my first beta buddy: sorry I forgot to include the airlocks.

Kurt Brown, my best friend of twenty years: go on, try to ruin this.

My dad, Tetter Rogers: not sure this passes the airport test.

Noel Rogers, my amazing brother: freedom *is* the right of all sentient beings.

Butcher the Doll (original)

I push through the downtrodden masses toward the brothel, thinking *this is my last kill.*

A hundred times I've told myself this lie, but murder is my primary programming.

I gaze at the tenement where my target is likely enjoying himself—unaware his end approaches—then grab the fire escape ladder and hoist myself up.

· · · ·

MY BOSS CHIANG—THE self-declared queen of the underworld—has directed me to terminate Quaid, a wealthy rival. I slip inside the cramped room of a renowned male Doll named Mix. My target is passed out, facedown and naked, snoring, content. No sign of Mix. The room smells of incense and sweat and droidsex.

I retrieve the gun from my waistband and fire through an oversized pillow into Quaid's skull. Feathers swirl around my face.

That's it. I'm done.

I'm swatting away errant feathers when Mix appears from the washroom. Dolls are attractive by design, but my breath catches at the sight of this perfect model. Still, I point my weapon at him.

Mix doesn't flinch, appearing more infuriated than frightened, shifting his glare from me to Quaid's corpse. "What the fuck?"

I've aimed this pistol in dozens of faces. Never have I encountered someone so unruffled; even ice-hearted Butchers like me beg for their lives.

Mix yanks the ruined pillow from Quaid's body and hurls it toward me. More feathers float through the room like a confusing snow. "Fuck you, Butcher, coming in here, killing my whale. Who sent you?"

"Chiang." I call her my boss, but she's technically my owner. It's not my job to care, but I note despair in Mix's gray-blue eyes. "You're not scared of me?"

Mix snorts. "You? Get the fuck out." He points towards the door.

· · · ·

CHARLIE ROGERS

A FRIGID RAIN ASSAULTS me when I leave the brothel. Most Butchers don't experience sensations like cold or pain, but I do. Chiang says I'm defective, but I suspect she knows otherwise. Still, other Butchers don't require comfort so she refuses to lodge me.

My tent beneath the bridge is filled with squatters. A shaggy pup gazes at me with trusting, hopeful eyes, a lizard stuffy in its mouth.

No dry locations remain. I'm facing a long, miserable night.

I locate a paltry shelter beside a long-dead tree, shivers wracking my body. I abandon any pretense that I'll sleep but close my eyes anyway.

When I open them, a familiar face glares above me.

"Well, if it isn't my least favorite Butcher... remember these?" Mix clutches his blood-spattered bedsheets. He inhales from a long, purple vaportube. "Thought I'd donate to the needy. Truly didn't expect that to be you."

"Leave me alone." I draw my knees to my chest.

He cocks his flawless face to one side. "No lodging at all?"

I shake my head.

He sighs. "Typical. Got a name, handsome?"

"Bull." My voice quivers from the cold.

"You're shaking." He offers me a well-manicured hand. "C'mon."

• • • •

THERE'S NO EVIDENCE of the murder when we return to Mix's room, except a smattering of feathers—some bloodied—lining the floor.

"Excuse the mess. Some idiot destroyed my best pillows." Mix flashes a mischievous grin. "Lose the wet clothes. You'll shave off a whole life-cycle with that shivering."

I hesitate. "I can't—"

Mix rolls his eyes. "Damn right you can't afford me. Get naked, you muscled lug."

He studies me as I disrobe. A series of unfamiliar sensations bubble underneath my skin. Shame? Desire?

Mix continues to evaluate my nakedness, then undresses as well. He sets his soft fingers against my prickled skin.

Sparks fire along my spine. No one's ever touched me this way before. Never gently, nor with affection. "Why are you being... kind?"

Mix clambers onto the bed. "Sometimes a boy wants a monster in his bed? I don't know." I believe he *does* know, but he isn't saying.

I climb beside him and hastily cover myself with a blanket. "Quaid was your best client? Sorry."

Mix's eyes bore into me, like I'm a puzzle he's trying to solve. He drags from his vaportube. "I was skimming from him to buy out my contract from Chiang. Freedom's the dream, right? His account locked as soon as he flatlined. But that's dull. Am I wrong that you want to kiss me?"

I'm not supposed to experience desire. I already feel plenty that other Butchers don't.

Mix leans in. "You're not what they say you are."

"What am I, then?"

Mix tugs at the sheet covering me and runs his palm across my knee. "You're like me. A Doll. I pegged it when you wagged that gun in my face... I saw sadness. Butchers don't show emotion."

Fuck. It makes sense.

Chiang called me defective. She knew the truth all along.

"And Butchers are never... handsome. You've been over-programmed."

My eyes lock his. "That why you brought me here?"

"No." Mix laughs. "You looked beyond pathetic, shivering out there. I watch out for our kind."

He smells of citrus and rain.

"There's a sweetness to you, Bull, whether you want it or not." Mix slides a curious hand further up my leg.

This time it's me who leans forward. I've never felt a man's—even another droid's—lips against mine before. The sensation overwhelms me. I feel alive.

• • • •

IN THE MORNING, MIX invites me to stay longer but offers me dry clothes when I explain I have a mission to complete. I feel like a different person in his bright-colored pants and shiny, form-fitting shirt.

I cross town to visit Chiang in her high rise. She'll likely have a new assignment for me, a new job for me to claim will be my last.

"What are you *wearing*?" She sprawls under an ultraviolet lamp. With one hand, she gestures me closer. With the other, she directs one of her multiple bodyguards to refill her cocktail.

I always knew who my last kill would be. A single bullet can free everyone under Chiang's thumb. Mix and a dozen of his kind. My kind. I reach for my gun a final time.

· · · ·

AUTHOR'S NOTE: THIS is the original, unmodified story I submitted to the Writing Battle competition in February, 2024. For the expanded version, I changed Quaid's name to Wade to prevent confusion with the new character Quentin. Why didn't I name Quentin something else, you ask? Sadly, I have no answer to that.

About the Author

C harlie Rogers (he/him) is a gay writer, former photographer and aspiring hermit who lives in New York City, writing the same story over and over, ignoring birds and their portents. He is originally from Beacon, NY, and studied literature at Cornell University for some reason. His writing has appeared in *Drunk Monkeys, Intrinsick*, and several TLDR anthologies, including *Breathless and Hope.*

9 798224 686407